THE MYSTERIOUS WU FANG:
THE CASE OF THE SCARLET FEATHER

THE CASE OF
THE SCARLET
FEATHER

By Robert J. Hogan

ALTUS PRESS • 2017

CHAPTER 1
ROOM OF THE DRAGON

THE BACK of Wu Fang was toward the entrance of the underground room when the heavy door creaked. His tall, narrow-shouldered body turned at the sound. Eyelids raised a little, revealing the green hardness of his eyes a bit more clearly.

His yellow face, as usual with this Lord of Death, was expressionless.

A brown-skinned figure, dressed in the clothes of the Occident, slipped through the door with scarcely a sound. Wu Fang stood half turned, waiting. The brown-skinned one nodded.

"We have him, Master," he said in a voice barely above a whisper.

Wu Fang's cruel, thin lips smiled and his face assumed an almost kindly look. The head with the long, narrow face and high, wide forehead nodded down and up—once.

"That is good, Kirda," he breathed. "You are sure he is the right man? The one who will know?"

The brown man called Kirda hesitated.

"Yes," he said after a pause, "I am sure of it, Master."

Wu Fang's smile faded for a split second and he nodded again. Nodded that long, wide head down and back—once.

"That will be well—if you are correct," he said. "There must be no mistakes, Kirda."

The baby-faced beast leaped—straight for Hazard!

The heavy silk robe that was covered with embroidery rustled slightly as the yellow man turned further toward the door.

"Have him brought in, Kirda," Wu Fang ordered.

Kirda bowed and whirled toward the heavy door that had closed behind him. He touched a portion of the casing and the

great oak portal opened again. Opened slowly as though some giant hand were operating it.

Through the door came two figures. They were large-muscled brown men, much like Kirda, but obviously of a lower caste. They were stripped to the waist.

Between them they carried a senseless form with head lolling back. He was a white man. He was neither bound nor gagged. He was unconscious.

Wu Fang smiled with the indulgence of a mother looking upon a slumbering child.

"Ah," he said. "He sleeps." Then sharply to Kirda: "He is the one—you are sure of that?"

Again there was that very slight hesitation on the part of Kirda. But he nodded and said, "Yes, Master," like a man who had gone this far and must go on to the end.

Wu Fang turned and faced a golden thing that jutted out into the underground room. It was a gigantic dragon's head and before it hung a litter, suspended from the heavily tapestried ceiling.

The yellow fiend uttered no word. He simply nodded toward the litter.

The two brown, naked men strode forward. Without effort, they lifted the limp form to the litter and fastened it there, feet pointing toward the golden head. They removed the white man's shoes and stockings and stepped back. Wu Fang produced a tiny hypodermic needle from one of his flowing sleeves. The point of this he injected into the ankle of the unconscious man and pressed the small plunger home.

The reaction was instantaneous.

The white man moved slightly and then raised his head and stared about.

Two changes of expression crossed his face in quick succession. First, the baffled look of one who is lost, who can not get his bearings. Then, at sight of the yellow, grinning face with the green eyes his expression changed to one of shock and fear. His lips moved.

"Who—are you?" he gasped.

Wu Fang did not smile now.

"You do not know me?" he asked.

The white man shook his head with a frightened gesture.

"No," he said and again, "no. I never saw you before."

"Then," Wu Fang smiled now, "perhaps you could guess?"

"No, no," the man protested and now, in his greater excitement, he spoke with a marked foreign accent. "What am I doing here? I—"

"You are here, my friend," Wu Fang smiled, "in order that your tongue may have a little exercise."

The white man's face became more startled than ever. He began to struggle against the bonds that held him.

"I—I don't know what you mean!"

"I mean," Wu Fang said, moving savagely closer to the white face, "that I am Wu Fang. Does that mean anything to you?"

The white man's mouth dropped open. Then his lips moved but before he could speak—could do more than form the words "Wu Fang"—the yellow man continued.

"You have been brought here to tell of the five casks."

Now the face went ghastly white.

"No, no," he said quickly. "I—I do not know anything about them."

Wu Fang bowed and rubbed his long-nailed hands together slowly.

"Perhaps you have forgotten," he murmured. "It will be necessary to refresh your memory with the breath of the dragon."

"No, no," the man exclaimed now. "What are you going to do? I do not know anything about the five casks. I—"

WU FANG turned with that slow deliberation that drove his victims mad. He clapped his hands three times, then swung back and smiled.

"I am very sorry to be forced to submit you to this," he apologized. "But at times we must endure pain to appreciate our health. Now in a moment you will understand what I mean. There. Feel it?"

Agony flashed across the white man's face. His mouth opened, but he seemed unable to cry out or speak for a moment. Then he expelled a horrible, blood-curdling scream of pain.

"My feet. My feet. They are burning up!"

He writhed and wriggled insanely. But the bonds held tight. His screams increased so that they stretched out into one long, continuous note of mortal pain. "My feet—my feet!"

Wu Fang clapped his hands twice and smiled as before upon the tortured white face before him.

"And now, my friend," he said, "perhaps now that your feet have tasted the breath of the dragon, you will be able to tell me of the five casks. You will tell me where they are to be taken?"

But again the white man on the litter shook his head.

"I do not know where they are to be taken. I am only a secretary to one of those who—"

He broke off. Wu Fang held his hands as though he were

going to clap them again. The white man went on, screeching this time.

"I—I will tell you everything if you will spare me. I am only the secretary of a member of the ring. I know nothing of the five casks except that my employer is interested in them. That is all."

At that moment Wu Fang did several things at once. He shot a cold green glance at Kirda. He stepped backward from the litter. He clapped his hands four times quickly. And he said:

"It is a pity that living men talk and must therefore die."

A surge of fire swept out, completely enveloping the white man and the litter. When the flame receded into the dragon's nostrils, the white man's body was not in view. But the gigantic jaws of the dragon head moved up and down with a horrible crunching sound.

Wu Fang turned to Kirda. The brown man of high caste cringed before him.

"Master," he faltered, "I thought I was right, Master. I beg of you—"

But Wu Fang's eyes glowed with that sudden strange green light, and Kirda's voice trailed off. Without taking his eyes from the eyes of Kirda, Wu Fang's lips moved.

"Summon all of them," he said.

He waited. There were scurrying sounds that were scarcely sounds at all. It was more the feel of grotesque figures slipping away into shadows. Then one by one people began entering that strange underground chamber again—half naked men and neatly attired men—and three women. Lovely young women.

The mysterious Wu Fang.

Still Wu Fang did not take his eyes from that face of Kirda. He seemed to sense without looking that his agents who were here with him in New York's Chinatown were all present. His thin, cruel lips opened.

"Kirda, you have made an error," he said softly. "There is room among my agents for only one error."

Kirda appeared transfixed either with the terrible gaze of Wu Fang or by stark fear. He did not move.

With the abruptness of a hurtling lightning bolt, Wu Fang flung out his right arm; the great flowing sleeve slipped back. His long-nailed index finger pointed at Kirda and from his hand a tiny, wriggling serpent glinted dully as it turned in the weird light and fastened its fangs in Kirda's throat.

The brown man uttered a choked cry. The serpent bit more deeply. Seemed to be gnawing into the flesh for just an instant.

Even as Kirda dropped to the floor, Wu Fang turned and faced his other agents who stood motionless—frozen.

"I desire the one who knows the secret of the five casks," he said. "I will wait. But not for long."

And as they had come in, they left as silently. Wu Fang's green eyes were upon one of the three women as she turned.

"Mohra!" he uttered the name as though it was sweet like honey to his thin lips.

The dark, slim, graceful beauty turned. And as though she were obeying an impulse that was irresistible, she walked toward him.

"My little flower," Wu Fang smiled. "You are even more

beautiful than ever. I will have work for you tonight, Mohra. You will not fail me?"

The green glow showed in the widening eyes of the yellow man and the girl nodded slowly. She even smiled back at him.

"I am ready," she said.

"I will have need of your two friends, Val Kildare and Jerry Hazard," Wu Fang murmured. "You will find them for me. Either one will do if they are not together. You will go at once. Advise me of their whereabouts when you have found them."

A look of fear flashed into Mohra's lovely dark eyes.

"You are planning a—"

She stopped short for the green eyes were glowing again weirdly.

"Mohra," Wu Fang said gently, "when I know the secret of the five casks I will be all-powerful. I will destroy everyone who refuses to submit to my demands. And then you, perhaps, shall be the queen of the world. Will that be unpleasant?"

The girl seemed to have lost her fear; it was apparent that the glowing green eyes of the fiend had had their desired effect. Wu Fang leaned a little closer to her as he repeated ever so softly:

"Remember. Val Kildare and Jerry Hazard. You will go—at once."

CHAPTER 2
MURDER WARNING

IN THE lounge of the New York Press Club, two men sat in a far corner by themselves. The one was young. He was rather tall, with an athletic build and a smile that came easily and wholeheartedly to his face. That was Jerry Hazard, special international correspondent for the McNulty News Syndicate.

The other man was slightly taller and a bit older. He sat well down in his chair, completely relaxed with one long leg wound around the other in a characteristic posture. Where Hazard was quick in his words and actions and gave evidence of being a bit high strung at times, the other was the embodiment of utter calm. When he smiled, he did so with reservation and when he chuckled, the sound seemed to come from the pit of his stomach. When he talked, he spoke with a certain calm assurance that made one feel utter confidence in the man and his ability. That was Val Kildare, former federal agent, now, for the most part, working on his own.

Hazard took out a pack of cigarettes. He shook one out, tapped it on the back of his hand, and placed it between his lips. Kildare, without shifting his position, took a lighter from his vest pocket. A flame glowed and he extended his long arm toward Hazard. Then, when Hazard had his light, he replaced the lighter and puffed at his long, slim cigar.

"Things have been rather dull lately in the news business, haven't they, Hazard?" he asked.

Hazard nodded, then wrinkled his face in a smile of recollection.

"We haven't had anything nearly as exciting as that episode with Wu Fang," he admitted. "Just the usual routine stuff. You know, England writes a note to Germany—and Italy tells the League of Nations where they can go. I'm afraid we won't ever get another story with a kick to it like that Wu Fang case."

Kildare looked up quickly.

"Why?"

Hazard shrugged and smiled again.

"Well, I've an idea that yellow devil was finished off in the explosion at the steam house."

Kildare shook his head. "I wouldn't be too sure," he said firmly.

"Oh, I wasn't planning to bet any money on it," Hazard came back, "but then—" the smile faded from his face and he looked grave—"If that yellow fiend was in the building when the explosion came, it's a cinch he was done for."

"Possibly," Kildare admitted, "but don't forget that we were never sure he was there. I thought I saw him go in, but I wasn't certain. It might have been one of his agents."

He paused and studied Hazard's face. The newspaperman was looking down at the glowing end of his cigarette, looking at it very thoughtfully.

"That case," Kildare went on with his slow smile, "had a lot of attraction for you, didn't it? Or, perhaps I should say, one attraction."

Hazard started, "What was that?"

Kildare chuckled.

"I thought you wouldn't hear that one. You haven't been able to get your mind off that girl Mohra, have you?"

Hazard pursed his lips for a moment, then a slightly sheepish smile crossed his face.

"Well, Kildare, he said, "you've got to admit that she's about the most beautiful girl you ever saw in your life."

"And the most mysterious, too. I imagine that's part of her attraction."

Hazard shrugged. "Perhaps."

Kildare puffed at his long, slim cigar for a moment before he spoke again.

"Something happened just before I came up here," he said. "I haven't mentioned it because I didn't want you to get all steamed up about it."

Hazard glanced up quickly. "What? You haven't seen Mohra?"

Kildare shrugged. "I'm not sure. It was when I entered the Press Club about twenty minutes ago. I was almost in front of the entrance when I noticed a cab wheeling along the street in the opposite direction. It slowed as it passed me—that must have been what drew my attention to it. It was dark inside the cab, but I could distinguish the face of a girl. Just as the taxi passed, she turned and glanced at me. Then, almost immediately, she turned her face away again and the cab moved on."

Jerry Hazard was leaning forward in his chair, his face flushed with excitement. Kildare smiled more broadly.

"Take it easy, old man," he advised. "It probably wasn't Mohra, but it certainly did look like her."

Hazard hesitated before he asked a question.

"Did you see which way the cab turned when it got to the corner?"

Kildare shook his head.

"No. What difference would that have made? I might have followed, but it so happened that there were no vacant cabs in sight."

HAZARD SAT there tensely for a moment. Then he took a long breath and dropped back in his chair. He began nodding slowly.

"So that," he ventured, "is what makes you think that Wu Fang might be back in circulation."

"Possibly," Kildare admitted.

Hazard's lips tightened. "Well, I think you're wrong."

"You don't even think," Kildare charged, "that the girl has anything to do with Wu Fang, do you?"

"I can't think that," Hazard admitted. "Naturally, I hope she isn't hooked up with him, but the odds are against that hope. I'm sure enough of one thing, though. I don't think Mohra has ever worked with this yellow fiend of her own free will."

"I agree with you there," Kildare admitted.

The admission relieved Hazard. He brought out another cigarette and lighted it from the stub of the old one.

"Kildare," he said, "there's one thing that has never been quite clear in my mind. Do you remember those deadly little beasts and reptiles that Wu Fang used?"

Kildare smiled slightly. "Could I ever forget them?"

"Those things worked," Hazard continued, "almost as though they were human, and yet of course they weren't."

"I tried to explain my theory of it before," Kildare answered. "Wu Fang has two methods of making those deadly hybrids execute his commands. Some of them are probably trained to kill; the others are controlled by a sense of odor.

"There are certain odors that are hardly perceptible to the human sense of smell, but which have a very strong effect on animals, especially insects. It would be quite simple to control those animals, therefore, with an odor repugnant to them. We could protect ourselves against them if we knew what this odor was, because we could rub it on our bodies and they wouldn't come near us. There are other odors that are extremely attractive to them. For instance, a cat is attracted to catnip. If I wanted to kill you with one of these little beasts that are controlled by smell, I could—in a crowded elevator or theatre, or on the street—touch some part of your skin with an oil whose odor attracts them. The next step would be easy. It would be necessary only to turn the animal loose near you—and the little beast would do the rest."

Hazard shivered visibly. "That," he said, "is certainly a lovely thought to go to sleep on."

A page boy came walking through the lounge.

"A phone call for Mr. Kildare," he announced.

Leisurely, Kildare took the long cigar out of his mouth, unwound his legs, and got up out of his chair. He frowned.

"That's funny. Wonder who knows I'm here at your club?"

Jerry Hazard bit his lip. Kildare smiled.

"You have a hunch, haven't you?" he asked. "There's only one person who saw me come in here so far as I know." He shrugged. "At any rate, we'll find out."

Jerry Hazard walked with him through the lounge and into the hall where the telephone booths were situated. He waited outside the booth while Kildare picked up the receiver, spoke.

"Hello…. Yes, this is Kildare…. Yes, Val Kildare. Who is this?"

Hazard saw his friend suddenly tense and grow rigid as though his spine had changed into a band of steel.

"What?… I see. Don't you think this is rather an obvious trap? You don't expect me to step into it as easily as that, do you?… Yes, I have it. Pier thirty-four. Captain Atlee of the *S.S. Sussex,* just docked."

He slammed up the receiver and whirled to Hazard.

"Who do you think that was?" he asked.

Hazard hesitated.

"Not—not Mohra?"

"No," said Kildare. "Believe it or not, that was Wu Fang."

"Wu Fang!" exclaimed Hazard. "What did he want?"

Kildare smiled.

"You'd never guess in a thousand years. It looks as though the yellow devil has turned stool pigeon to help the law."

Hazard looked blank. "I don't get it."

"You wouldn't," Kildare hurried on. "Wu Fang phoned to tell me that a man is going to be murdered tonight."

Hazard's jaw dropped.

"Wu Fang," he repeated, "called to tell you someone is going to be murdered tonight?"

Kildare gave a short nod.

"Yes," he said. "That's right. At pier thirty-four. He said Captain Atlee of the *S.S. Sussex* is going to be killed. Hazard, Wu Fang is alive, and we're going to capture—or kill—him."

He turned abruptly and started for the check room, with the obvious purpose of getting his hat and coat. Hazard started after him.

"Listen, Kildare," he pleaded. "You can't go. This whole thing is a trap. Wu Fang wants to catch you and get you out of the way. He's got something up his sleeve."

Kildare nodded again. "I thought of that at once and told him so. He admitted that he expected me to think it was a trap, and he swears that it isn't. He told me there will be no attempt made on my life by either him or any of his agents before midnight, and he challenges me to come and see that this time he will keep his word."

"Good Lord!" breathed Hazard. "You aren't going to believe that, are you?"

"Certainly I am," Kildare nodded. "I'm going to try him out this once. Want to come along?"

Hazard quietly took down his hat and coat. "Nothing could stop me," he said.

They hurried outside, hailed a taxi and directed the driver to pier thirty-four.

"You see," Kildare smiled in the cab, "I was right about Wu Fang."

"Yes," Hazard breathed, "and about Mohra, too."

TEN MINUTES later the cab turned into a cross-town street. Bending down so he could see through the windshield, down the chasm between the high buildings on either side, Hazard saw a tall ship mast and smoke stacks looming ahead.

"That's the pier," Kildare snapped, "and that's The *Sussex*, too. She just docked tonight. I remember reading it in the paper this evening. She was due to come in about a half hour ago, and apparently, she was right on time."

They left the cab at the docks and ran through the warehouse and up the gangplank. An officer stopped them at the other end of the foot bridge. Kildare flashed his badge,* jerked his head toward Jerry Hazard.

"This is my friend, Hazard," he said. "We've got something very important to discuss with the captain at once. Where is he?"

The officer stepped back.

"I think you will find him in his cabin up forward on A deck," he said.

The hallway on the lower deck was piled high with baggage as passengers waited their turn for customs inspection. Hazard and Kildare picked their way past to one of the wide staircases.

---

* Although one of Wu Fang's agents in the Department of Justice had succeeded in having Val Kildare discharged on false evidence, Kildare had received permission from his immediate superior to retain his federal badge.

They sped up it—perhaps they were too late; perhaps the captain had already been killed. C deck—up to B—finally they found themselves on an open steel stairway leading to A deck.

A deck hand brushed past them.

"We must see the captain," Kildare said sharply.

The deck hand hesitated, then nodded.

"Yes, sir. I saw him a moment ago standing on the bridge."

"On the bridge?" Kildare repeated.

That was funny. The ship was in dock and the captain was still standing on the bridge. He continued up the stairs, ran forward to the bridge. The captain was standing with his back to them, standing quietly and alone, looking out over the great city with its shimmer of lights and the towers that stuck up into blackness. He turned slowly.

"Captain Atlee?" Kildare asked.

The man nodded.

"Yes," he said in a rather kindly voice, "what can I do for you?"

Kildare flashed his badge.

"I am Kildare, government agent," he said, lowering his voice. "Nothing has happened? You are quite all right?"

The captain smiled in a rather bewildered manner.

"Yes. Why?"

"Simply this," Kildare hurried on. "Don't be alarmed. I think it will be all right since we got here in time to tell you."

He repeated Wu Fang's warning. The captain's eyes narrowed. He stepped back against the rail instinctively, suddenly on guard.

"I don't quite understand, gentlemen," he said.

"It has me stumped, too," Kildare confessed.

"But what can it all be about?" the captain demanded.

"I had hopes," Kildare said, "that you could come closer to explaining that than we could. You just docked a short time ago, didn't you?"

"Yes, about a half hour ago."

"Did anything peculiar happen before you docked? I mean, did anything strange happen at all on the voyage over?"

The captain hesitated. He looked from Kildare to Hazard, then nodded.

"Yes," he said. "Something did happen. It has had me guessing."

"What was it?" demanded Kildare.

"It was this evening," the captain said. "It wasn't quite dark yet, but the sun had gone down. The watch aft reported a small fast cruiser coming from the north. He looked at it through his spy glass, but couldn't distinguish any name. He said the cruiser was traveling on a course that would just about cut past our stern. A moment later, he reported something very strange. It was—"

Suddenly, Hazard let out a shout of warning.

CHAPTER 3
THE FLOATING CASKS

KILDARE AND Hazard were standing directly in front of the captain, who was leaning against the back tail of the open bridge. In spite of the lights on the rest of the ship, it was rather dark up there, but just the same Hazard had seen something move.

It was something that climbed—a Roman figure that had crawled up the steelwork to a point just behind the railing.

"Look out!" he yelled.

At the same instant, the climbing figure leaped up. One arm rose and fell like a blur in the darkness. Hazard jumped forward.

In the wild jumble of sound and action, few things were clear to him but he knew the hand of that climber had descended with terrific force. He heard a thud—something gleamed in the darkness, reflecting the lights of the city and the docks.

Then Hazard had the climber by the wrist, the one with which he was grasping the rail. He tried to hang on, but the attacker wrenched free. The sudden pull jerked Hazard against the rail which caught him in the ribs; his breath was suddenly expelled.

The man landed on the lower deck. Hazard caught a good glimpse of him as he fell—but the glimpse was only momentary. He couldn't see much except that the man was hatless and wore a business suit of average tailoring. He tried to yell, but the breath had been jerked out of him and he couldn't move, much less speak. He stood there, half paralyzed, gasping.

He saw the captain fall forward with a groan, saw Kildare catch him. Then someone leaped past him. Having lowered the captain to the floor of the bridge, Val Kildare was hurdling the rail in one wild leap after the murderer. He flung an order over his shoulder as he dropped to the lower deck.

"Get the ship's doctor! I'll be back."

Hazard caught his breath enough to shout out now. "Help! Get the ship's doctor up here on the bridge."

Then he knelt down beside the captain. The captain was breathing with a rasping, gurgling sound. A knife was sticking out of his back just above where his heart should be.

Grabbing the handle, he drew it straight out. A groan came from the wounded man. Hazard stared at the knife, in perplexity. That was funny. It wasn't a dagger such as one would expect in connection with Wu Fang, but a butcher knife, a regular case knife with a blade almost a foot long, such as might he used in the galley of the ship.

The captain was moving feebly now, trying to utter words. Hazard bent lower.

"Yes, captain," he encouraged, "what is it? I'm listening."

The captain was trying to make himself clear, but his words were just a jumble, of sounds that were thick with the blood that was oozing from his mouth. There was only one word Hazard could understand and that he wasn't positive of; it sounded like casks.

Then someone was running up the steel steps; lights appeared on the bridge and a ship's officer ran forward, a little black case in his hand.

"I'm the ship's doctor," he explained. "What's wrong?"

Hazard leaped to his feet and stepped back out of the way.

"Captain Atlee," he said. "He's been stabbed. I don't—"

He stopped short as the doctor stooped over the form of the captain. After a moment he looked up, saw the knife that Hazard was holding.

"That?" he demanded.

Hazard nodded. The doctor shook his head.

"It must have gone in him almost a foot. It's a wonder it didn't come out the other side."

Quickly he tore the clothing away from the captain's back, examined the wound. He shook his head again.

"I'm afraid we're too late. Help me turn him over."

Hazard helped with his free hand. He didn't want to lay that knife down and take a chance of spoiling any identification marks on it.

THEY TURNED the captain over on his back and the doctor forced the eyelids open. Then he uttered a curse, clenching his teeth as he did so.

"I'd like to have the murderer that did this," he choked. "There wasn't a better man living than Captain Atlee."

"He's dead?" Hazard asked in a low voice.

The ship's doctor nodded. "Any idea who did it?"

"It happened right before us. My friend and I were talking with the captain when someone slipped up behind him. The lights were off and I didn't get a good look at him."

"You wouldn't know him again if you saw him?" the doctor asked savagely.

Hazard frowned.

"I don't know," he said. "Kildare ought to be back any minute."

"Val Kildare?" asked the doctor. "Was he with you?" Hazard nodded.

"If Kildare is on the case, we'll find out who did it," the doctor said.

As he finished speaking, Val came running up the stairs to the bridge.

"Did you get him?" Hazard shouted.

The Secret Service man shook his head.

"No. If I had had my gun, I could have winged him, but be got away. Went over the side. He can't escape, though. I've got the harbor police searching the docks and they'll get him when he tries to get ashore. What about the captain?"

"He's dead," Hazard told him and introduced him to the doctor.

"I have heard a great deal about you, Kildare," the doctor admitted, holding out his hand, "and I am sure of one thing. If there's anyone who can catch the murderer of Captain Atlee, it is you."

"Thank you," said Kildare. "I hope you won't have occasion to lose that faith. Now what's been going on here since I left?"

"This for one thing," Hazard said, displaying the knife which he still clutched between his thumb and forefinger.

"That's a funny thing," Kildare said. "From the looks of that chap that I chased, I rather expected to find an ugly-looking dagger. But this is an ordinary kitchen knife."

He took the weapon in his own hands, handling it the same way Hazard had.

"Why, look here," he said. "The name of the ship is right on the handle—*S. S. Sussex*, burned in the wood. That's mighty queer. If the cook or one of the galley men did this job, we would have a perfectly open and shut case."

"Sure," Hazard nodded. "I can see the headline now. 'Kitchen attendant aboard *S. S. Sussex* kills captain for hate.'"

"Fine," agreed Kildare. "But the man that did the job was no kitchen mechanic. Well, what else happened since I went over the rail?"

"The captain tried to tell me something," Hazard went on, "but he died before he could get it all out. He said something about casks or caskets."

Kildare turned to the ship's doctor.

"Do you know anything about this?" he asked. "Have you any idea what he might have meant?"

The doctor looked bewildered.

"No, I haven't the slightest idea," he confessed.

Kildare frowned, then suddenly his face brightened. "I think I know how we can find out. That is, if another member of the crew hasn't been killed also. Do you remember what the captain was saying?"

"Yes, but—"

"He was talking about something odd that happened at twilight this evening," Kildare raced on. "The after watch had reported a fast cruiser coming from the north. He said that the cruiser would just about cut the stern and then the watch reported something—very strange."

"Yes," Hazard nodded. "He didn't finish that, did he? It was just then that the killer stuck the knife in his back."

By now, several ship's officers had gathered on the bridge and on the forward part of A deck. Kildare gave a short nod and turned to them.

"Men," he said, in a low voice: "your captain has been murdered. Who is the next in command?"

A well-built officer stepped up.

"I'm the first officer," he announced. "Is there something I can do? I'd do anything to get the—"

Kildare cut him off with, "Yes, there is something you can do. Issue an order that no one is to leave the ship. Station your men around the rails to see that no one jumps overboard. Then assemble all the men in your cabin who have been on watch for the last few hours. Particularly, I want the watch on the after part of the ship—the man who was on duty at twilight tonight."

The first officer nodded.

"I'll see to it at once," he nodded and turning, ran down to B deck.

WHEN KILDARE and Hazard entered the cabin of the first officer, some ten minutes later, several members of the crew were already present. Outside, the searchlights combed black river waters and on every deck men were stationed, guarding the rails to watch that no one escaped.

Kildare glanced around at the weather-beaten faces before him.

"Men," he began, "you probably all know about your captain being murdered tonight." Heads nodded solemnly. "The reason I called you here," he went on, "is to ask a question. Which one of you men was on the after watch at twilight?"

A husky, raw-boned Scandinavian stood up.

"I was, sir."

Kildare studied him for a moment then nodded.

"The captain told us," he said, "that you reported a fast cruiser about to cross your course from the north."

"That's right, sir."

"The captain also stated that you reported this cruiser, if it held to its course, would just about cut your stern."

"That's right, sir."

"Then," said Kildare, "he was about to tell us something else, but at that moment he was stabbed. Can you tell us what he was going to say?"

"I think so," the seaman nodded. "I was on the after watch and I saw this cruiser. She was very fast and she was coming from the north, like the captain said. I looked through my glass, but I couldn't see a name on her. I thought at first she was a fishing cruiser, but she was too fast. She slowed up or she would have crossed our stern about a hundred feet back. Then I saw five casks floating in the water. They were like wine comes in. Maybe they would each hold five gallons. They were bobbing all together there on the waves.

"I reported at once to the captain by telephone, told him that I thought somebody had thrown the casks out of the hold. They floated like maybe they were half full. As we went on, I saw the cruiser stop and pick them up. I tried to shout to them and tell them not to do it, but they didn't pay any attention to me."

Kildare nodded.

"Have you any idea what was in those casks?"

The seaman shook his head.

"No, sir, but it's probably all down in the ship's file of cargo. I imagine the captain intended to check that."

"H'm," Kildare said. "Five casks. That's funny. And you say they were thrown overboard just about twilight?"

"Yes, sir."

"That would be about forty miles out of the harbor," he ventured.

"Yes, sir."

"And the cruiser was coming from the north—that would mean from the south side of Long Island. Did you see which way it went after it picked up the casks?"

"Yes, sir," said the other. "It turned and headed out to sea."

"H'm," said Kildare. "Rather looks as if they wanted to cover up their tracks. Did the captain—"

Suddenly, he stopped short. Through the open porthole just behind him, a sound had cut the night. It was a wild, terror-stricken scream.

As he listened, the sound came again, shrill and penetrating above the jumble of noise emulating from the docks and the great city beyond.

Kildare whirled for the door, tore it open and dived through it. Hazard was right behind him. As he raced into the corridor he almost collided with a figure moving along the hall, a figure with a little black case in his hand. It was the ship's doctor.

"Come on, doctor," Kildare shouted. "Did you hear that scream?"

"Yes," the doctor shot back. "I think it came from the wharfs."

The three of them ran down to the gangplank and up the loading platforms to the street. Skirting the piers, they joined a cop who was also running.

"Which way?" Kildare shouted in a voice of authority.

The cop pointed farther down the street, in the direction he was heading.

"Down there somewhere," he gasped. "Sounds like somebody's been murdered."

They ran on together, Kildare, Hazard, the ship's doctor, and the police officer, until they reached the third pier where a crowd was gathered. Cops were trying to keep back the mob. Kildare pushed the police officer ahead of him.

"Go ahead," he said. "You can break through the line better."

Then they were all crowding through the morbid throng of curiosity seekers. In the center of a little circle of citizens and police, a still figure lay on the pavement.

Kildare flashed his badge so that the cops could see. "Now," he said, "what happened here? Who saw this?"

An officer on the other side of the body spoke up.

"I guess I was here first," he said, "but I didn't see it happen. I don't think anybody did. It's pretty dark at this corner of the warehouse and I was about a hundred feet away when I heard him scream. I saw him reeling around and fighting like he was shadow boxing a ghost. There wasn't anybody there, only him. And then, a second or so later, he let out another yell and fell, right here where he lays now."

CHAPTER 4
THE HAND OF WU FANG

KILDARE JERKED his head to the ship's doctor. "Let's see what we can find," he said.

The doctor opened his case and took out a flashlight. The man had slumped in a queer, twisted position on his back. The surgeon made a hasty examination.

"He's dead all right," he said, "stone dead, but I can find no wound, of any kind."

They rolled the man over on his face. Suddenly, Kildare tensed.

"Wait," he exclaimed. "Hold that flashlight there. That's it, at the back of his head."

Leaning down, he touched the corpse's left ear and pulled it forward a little; then he pointed behind it.

"See that?" he asked.

"Where?" the doctor demanded.

"I see it," Hazard put in. "Two marks very close together."

"You mean those two pimples?" the doctor inquired.

"They may be pimples to you," Kildare said, "but—" He took the skin and squeezed it between his thumb and forefinger. "See that?"

A very tiny speck of blood oozed out from each of the infinitesimal skin abrasions that the doctor had referred to as pimples. Kildare looked up at the police officer who had been the first to arrive.

"I think," he said, "if you will tell the coroner to have tests

30

made of the fluid that comes out of those two little wounds, you will find snake venom."

"Snake venom! But I just got through telling you, so help me; the fellow was trying to fight off a ghost or something. He was shadow boxing like a fool and there wasn't anything around him. I'll swear there wasn't a snake near him. I didn't see one."

"No, it wasn't meant that you should see one," Kildare said. "It was too small. There's just one thing more."

He took a fountain pen out of his pocket and turned to Hazard. "Which hand was it that the murderer of the captain held the knife in?"

Hazard thought for a minute.

"It was his left hand," he decided, "because he was holding on to the rail with his right and that was the one I grabbed."

Kildare picked up the left hand of the dead man and pressed the fingers against the black rubber sides of the pen; then he wrapped the instrument in his handkerchief and stood up.

Hazard followed him as he pushed on through the crowd and walked to the nearest street lamp. Here he produced a tiny box of powder and sprinkled some of it lightly over the fountain pen and the knife handle. He blew off the powder then and even in the dim light of the street lamp, the finger prints on both the handle and the fountain pen were quite apparent. A folding magnifying glass enabled him to study them more clearly. He made a brief examination. At length, he nodded with satisfaction.

"That's him all right."

Hazard stared.

"That's who?" he demanded.

"The murderer," Kildare said softly.

"You mean," demanded Hazard, "that this fellow who was just killed is the man who murdered Captain Atlee?"

Kildare nodded.

"But why?"

"Never mind that now," Kildare snapped. "Let's get out of here."

He led the way, pushing through the throng that had collected about the street lamp. Hazard handed back the fountain pen and Kildare stuffed it into his pocket. He held the knife in his fingers as he had before, being careful not to smudge the finger-prints on the handle.

They were halfway out of the crowd when Hazard felt a jerk on his coat. His first thought was of pickpockets. He turned instantly in an effort to catch the thief, but he saw no suspicious face. The crowd was beginning to move on now. There were only backs turned toward him—the backs of an average New York throng.

Many thoughts flashed through his mind. Why had someone tugged at his coat? If it had been a pickpocket, he had certainly bungled the job. There was nothing to pick in that pocket because all he usually carried in it was a handkerchief.

Suddenly, a thought, much more sinister flashed into his mind. He remembered what Kildare had said about these tiny murdering beasts of Wu Fang and how he believed them to be controlled by a sense of smell. Had someone just touched him with the scent that would attract one of these deadly things? The idea gave him a queer feeling along his spine.

He was still staring back. Suddenly he got a glimpse of something—a flash of a head and shoulders in the light of a street lamp, the back of a head under a trim, little hat. The next instant it was gone—head, shoulders, and all. A name formed on his lips.

"Mohra!"

WHIRLING, HE dashed through the throng, jostling, pushing. He was under the street light, tearing on, going like mad. He searched faces, but the throng had grown so that it half blocked the street

"Hazard! Hazard!" It was Kildare's voice. "Where are you?"

Hazard managed to choke back, "Here," and went on searching. But the hunt was fruitless. Out of all those faces there wasn't one that was familiar. A strange feeling grasped him when he returned to Kildare, who was staring at him.

"What's the matter with you, man?" Kildare demanded. "You look as though you'd seen a ghost."

"I saw Mohra," Hazard said. "I'm sure I did."

"Mohra?" gasped Kildare. "Where?"

"Back in the crowd under the light." He jerked his head in the direction he mentioned.

"You mean you just happened to bump into her?" Kildare demanded.

"No, not exactly," Hazard said. "Apparently, she didn't want me to see her. When we were pushing through the crowd somebody jerked my right coat pocket. I thought instantly of a pickpocket, then I thought of what you said about Wu Fang's killer beasts and how they may be governed by their sense of smell. Suddenly I was sure I saw Mohra's head and shoulders— but I lost her in the crowd. I can't figure—"

Kildare was smiling, smiling in slow amusement.

"I may be wrong," he said, "but the first thing you thought of was that someone had tried to pick your pocket. Why not reverse that idea and figure that someone was putting something in your pocket rather than taking it out? That would seem more logical, wouldn't it?"

Hazard looked dumbfounded.

"Why, I never thought of that. After I saw Mohra, I guess I lost all my senses."

As he spoke, he plunged his hand into his coat pocket. His expression of amazement increased as he drew out a folded piece of paper, Kildare snatched it. They had reached another street lamp by then and he began opening the paper. He read it half aloud:

> The men you seek in connection with the murder of Captain Atlee are about to escape from stern of S.S. *Sussex*. They will be taken by a small boat to the end of Pier 27 where a car will meet them. Perhaps you will be interested to know that they belong to a European spy ring. Your friend until midnight,
>
> Wu-Fang.

The instant that Kildare had finished reading, he struck off on a dead run for pier thirty-four. Once across the gangplank, he shouted for the first officer at the top of his voice.

THE CASE OF THE SCARLET FEATHER

A portly dowager, eyes ablaze, stepped out of the throng of passengers gathered at the inner end of the gangplank.

"Young man," she said to Kildare, "are you responsible for our being detained on this ship? Anyone would think that we are all suspected of murder. I want you to understand that I have a very important reception to attend, I am due there right now."

"Sorry," said Kildare as he pushed past her, "but I'm afraid you'll have to wait."

The flabby muscles of the dowager's face twitched and her eyes blazed hotter than ever.

"Young man," she puffed, "do you know who I am?"

Kildare shook his head. "You might be the queen of France, but it wouldn't make any difference."

Then he was dashing to the upper deck, calling as he went for the first officer. He found him amidships.

"Here," he said, "before I go any farther, I want to give you this." He handed him the knife. "Be careful of the handle. There are valuable finger-prints on it. You will find they were made by the man we heard scream a few minutes ago. Has anybody left this ship?"

"Not that I know of," the first officer said. "It was reported a moment ago that a launch came close to the stern. My men drove it away."

Kildare gave a short nod. "That stern is all dark. The water around the rest of the ship is plainly lighted. Quick! We've got to get to pier 27 and stop them."

The first officer looked blank.

"How do you know where they're going?" he demanded.

"Because we got a note telling us so and I haven't any reason to doubt the authenticity of it. Come with us if you like. You'll be interested, I think."

THEY RAN down the gangplank again and out into the street. News about the captain's murder and of the other death had traveled swiftly. A police car was just skidding to a stop at the end of the wharf. Kildare hailed it and flashed his badge.

"Quick!" he ordered "Pier twenty-seven. I'll tell you about it as we go." He glanced around at the dim light.

"I guess you couldn't read this note," he said to the first ship officer who had crowded in beside him, "so I'll tell you what it said."

He repeated to him, then, the contents of the note. The officer frowned.

"You know," he said. "We didn't get a chance to tell you the rest of that story about the five casks. The captain and some of the crew went down into the hold immediately and caught three of the passengers just slipping away."

"Were there more than five casks in the shipment?" Kildare asked.

"No, only five," came the answer. "These three men were caught. But the captain couldn't get a thing out of them by questioning them, so he decided to lock them up in the brig and turn them over to the authorities when we landed. I believe when you came on the bridge, he was waiting for the police. But how they could escape off the stern is more than I know.

And whoever it was that tipped you off with this note is very clever indeed."

"Clever," said Kildare, "is no word for it." He leaned over to the officer driving the police car.

"Here's pier twenty-seven right ahead. There's a cab drawn up before it now."

He turned to the first officer quickly. "By the way, the name and address of the man to whom those casks were being shipped is on your freight list, isn't it?"

The first officer nodded. Kildare scribbled a telephone number on a piece of note paper and handed it to him.

"I would appreciate it if you would phone me up when you get back to the ship and give me his name and address."

As he finished speaking the police car pulled up beside the waiting taxi. Kildare leaped out and confronted the driver.

"Are you waiting for somebody?" he asked.

The driver nodded. "Yes, sir."

"Who?"

"I don't know. The company got a radiogram telling them to have a cab at this time at pier twenty-seven."

"O.K.," Kildare nodded. "You'll have passengers all right. Stick around." He turned to the driver of the police car.

"Better pull up out of sight around the other cab," he ordered. "I want one of you cops to hide on the off side of the cab in case we arrest the gang. I would like to have the other go with us. It so happens that I haven't a gun."

The car moved on and parked in the shadow beyond. Then the two patrol car cops came back. One crouched on the running board of the cab. The other went down the pier with Kildare, Hazard, and the ship's officer.

It was dark down there, dark as pitch. No ships were docked here. They had to pick their way cautiously as they walked. Halfway down the pier, Kildare stopped.

"Listen," he said, "there's a boat pulling in. Quick! Back against the wall!"

The four men crouched low in the pitch blackness of the overshadowing wall of the wharf. They heard a boat, approaching slowly. The motor was running quietly, making very little noise. It came closer and closer.

CHAPTER 5
THE CLOCK STRIKES TWELVE

HAZARD TRIED to see over the edge of that wharf, tried to see the occupants of the small boat that was pulling alongside. But it was pitch dark and there were no dock lights nearby. He could see nothing except a blurry shadow. The boat was almost alongside now. He stuck out his hand to hold the others back until he gave the signal.

They heard mumbling in some foreign tongue. Hazard recognized it instantly—French. He saw a man's head and shoulders rise above the level of the dock. An instant later the figure heaved himself over the side. Turning, he bent down on his hands and knees. Another man appeared and then another. The first one was helping the rest up.

Three, four men. They were speaking English now. Two of them spoke with a French accent.

"Ah, at last we are safe!"

Hazard moved slightly, getting ready to spring, but Kildare's hand still held him back.

"*Jawohl!*" answered a guttural voice, deep and vibrant. "The cab is waiting."

A third man leaned over the edge. Apparently, there was a fifth person still in the launch.

"You will return, Louis," he said. "We go to follow the—"

"Ssh," the fourth man counseled gently. "There is perhaps someone listening."

The man addressed as Louis said, "I get you. I've got to stop and get some gas for this tub, but I'll be out there before morning."

"Good," nodded the third man. "You will tell them to wait until we arrive. It may be one or two days. From the address given, it may be hard to find."

Hazard was sure now. This would be the time to strike. Was Kildare going to let this launch get away?

The launch was moving from the dock, the old one-lung engine puffing softly in the darkness. Once more, Hazard prepared to leap forward, but again Kildare's hand held him back.

The four men had turned and started walking up the dock on tip-toe. Hazard couldn't contain himself any longer. He whirled to Kildare, got his lips close to his ear.

"Aren't you going to try to stop them?" he demanded.

"No," Kildare hissed back. "Something more important. Wait ten seconds, then follow them. Let them get in the cab. The cop out there on the running board ought to be able to take care of them. I'll join you later."

Suddenly he moved away, crouched over, toward the river end of the dock. They heard the muffled sound of the launch purring out in the river. Hazard counted ten slowly.

"Seven, eight, nine, ten," he finished. "Come on. Officer, keep your gun ready. I have an idea these men won't surrender any too easily."

The cop nodded. "I'll take care of them."

Out at the land end of the pier, they saw the dull glow of a street lamp and there, silhouetted against the light, the four men sauntered. The tail end of the taxi was sticking out beyond the corner of the building.

"If they get in from this side," Hazard whispered, we're all set."

The four men walked faster as they neared the taxi. Hazard quickened his pace and the others followed. One of the men was speaking to the driver; another was going around to the back of the car.

Hazard broke into a wild burst of speed.

"Quick!" he said, "it will all be over in a second unless we get there in time. That one bird is going around to the side where the cop is hiding on the running board."

As he spoke, they searched the corner of the wharf where it fronted on the street. At the same instant a cry of alarm sounded from the outer side of the car.

THE CASE OF THE SCARLET FEATHER

"Mon Dieu! Coures! Coures! C'est un home!"

They heard another cry, too. It was the bellow of the hidden cop.

"Don't move, any of you!" the cop yelled.

BUT THE warning didn't seem to have any effect on the three men who still stood on the wharf side of the taxi. There was a wild scramble. One, a stout fellow, whirled and headed south. A slim, gaunt man turned north and the third headed back along the wharf the way he had just come—only to bump face to face with Hazard.

Hazard grabbed him. There was a wild struggle and flailing of arms; then he pushed him toward the first officer. A big, weather-beaten fist came slamming up into the fugitive's face.

As Hazard turned and started for the second man, he saw the little fellow pitch backwards, unconscious.

A shot rang out in the night. The gaunt man turned quickly. He was making good time, but Hazard was gaining on him. He broke off to the left and headed across the street. Hazard cut across the angle. Making a wild leap through the air, he struck out with his arms and shoulders.

The gaunt one went down, kicking and struggling. He managed to get one foot free and with a terrific kick, planted it against those sore ribs where earlier in the evening, Hazard had been jerked against the rail of the bridge.

Hazard grunted and the breath went out of him, but he managed to hang on. The man tried to kick again, but Hazard was upon him and his fists were pounding that face with all the strength he possessed. The struggles of the gaunt man slowly decreased. Those blows of Hazard's had told heavily on him.

"Monsieur, monsieur," he pleaded. "Do not hit me again."

Hazard got up. "O.K.," he said. "Sit up on your hind legs. Now walk ahead of me to that taxi. I should have shot you first, but if you try to escape again, I will plug you, so help me."

He doubled up his forefinger and shoved the knuckle against the man's back. The gaunt man flinched.

"Monsieur," he faltered. "I—" He broke off suddenly.

"Go on. What were you going to say?" Again, Hazard prodded him in the back with his knuckle.

"I don't want you to shoot me, *monsieur.*"

"You won't get shot as long as you behave yourself," muttered Hazard.

Peering ahead in the dim light of that one street lamp, he saw the first officer pushing the little fellow into the taxi. From down the street the other cop was coming; he carried the form of a man over his shoulder.

"Yeah," the cop said as Hazard and his prisoner reached the cab, "I had to wing this guy in the leg to stop him. What will we do with this gang?"

"Put them in the cab," Hazard ordered.

As he spoke, he jabbed his prisoner again in the back with his knuckle.

"Get in there," he commanded.

The man obeyed readily.

A moment later all four men were in the rear of the taxi and the door slammed shut on them. A cop stood on either running board.

Just then Kildare came running around the corner of the wharf. He called the nearest cop and Hazard heard him say something in a low voice.

"That launch has got to be followed," he was whispering. "It's heading down river—to someplace on the Long Island shore, I think. Your job is to get hold of the river police and describe the launch to them as best you can. Tell them to follow it no matter where it goes. Then report to headquarters. We'll drive your car back."

The cop gave a short nod.

"Right, sir," he said. Then he was gone.

Kildare glanced inside the cab, studied the faces of their four prisoners. He turned to the driver.

"Take these men to headquarters," he said. "You, officer, ride beside the driver. Keep your gun on these four every minute. They're desperate and are apt to do almost anything."

The cop hesitated before he asked, "What have they done?"

"Enough to hold them for quite a while," Kildare nodded. "My tip was that they belong to an international spy ring. See that they get to headquarters. We'll follow in your car. I'll make the charges when we get there."

AT HEADQUARTERS, the police surgeon was called to treat the big fellow's bullet-blasted leg. The others seemed to be in fair enough physical condition. At Kildare's suggestion, the first officer repeated the story of Captain Atlee's murder. When he had finished the police captain nodded.

"So three of these men were locked up in the brig on charges of stealing those five casks," he asked.

"Yes," the first officer said. "Those are the three."

He pointed to the big fellow, the gaunt man, and the little one. "As for him—" he gestured toward the fourth, a ratty little man with a pinched face—"I remember him as one of the passengers."

The captain turned sternly to one of the police officers in the room.

"Search the prisoners," he ordered.

The cop began a systematic search of their clothing. He took out papers, jack knives, odds and ends of all descriptions and laid them in separate piles on the captain's desk. The ratty little man, who was last, objected.

"This is ridiculous," he fumed. "You can't search us like this. You have made a mistake. We were returning from a fishing trip on that launch."

Kildare smiled, "It isn't often that an open, one-lung fishing boat sends a wireless message to a taxi cab company requesting a cab to meet them at an empty dock."

"Here's something," the cop who was searching him shouted as he pulled out a large bunch of keys.

The ship's officer stared at them, then took them in his hand for closer examination.

"I think this answers quite a lot," he said slowly. "This bunch of keys belonged to the captain. He usually kept it hanging behind the door in his cabin."

He turned to the ratty little man and pointed his finger

accusingly at him. "You knew," he rasped, "that Captain Atlee was going to be murdered at a certain time and you slipped into his cabin while everything was in confusion and got this bunch of keys with which you released the three prisoners."

The man glared back, but seemed to have nothing to say.

"That," Kildare decided, "seems to tie up these men convincingly with the murder."

The police captain nodded.

"What other charges?"

"In the first place," Kildare enumerated on his fingers, "they are suspected of belonging to a European spy ring. That's just a tip I received. It won't be any good as evidence. In the second place, this man stole that bunch of keys in conjunction with the captain's murder."

"That's a lie," cried the ratty man. "I didn't have anything to do with the murder."

"Only," said Kildare, "that the murder was perhaps put on especially so that you would have a chance to get into the captain's cabin."

"You're crazy," snarled the other. "I—" Then he stopped suddenly.

"Those charges," Kildare went on, "are for the courts governing marine crime to decide. The other thing is a matter for the immigration and customs authorities to take up. These men left the *S. S. Sussex* without permission of the authorities."

"It looks," said the captain, "as if they will be behind the bars for quite a while."

"Yes," Kildare nodded, "but I want to be sure of at least one thing. I don't want them to see anyone for twenty-four hours."

The wizened little man spoke up angrily.

"We know our rights," he said. "We've got a right to consult an attorney."

Kildare was thinking fast, but Hazard beat him to it.

"I think you're right," Hazard said, winking at the captain so that the four prisoners couldn't see him.

"Officer," he said, addressing the cop who had ridden with the four men in the cab. "Didn't you see a sign saying 'No Trespassing' on pier twenty-seven?"

The cop grinned. "Sure, these fellows weren't supposed to land there. They didn't have any authority."

"Then," said Hazard, addressing the captain again, "these men can be held without counsel for twenty-four hours on charges of vagrancy. Isn't that right?"

"Sure," the captain nodded. "That's right."

Kildare smiled. "I guess that settles it for tonight, captain. You might as well lock them up and we'll go home."

The four men were ushered out of headquarters office through a back door in the prison cells. Kildare glanced toward the outer door that led to the street.

"I would like to see that other officer before we go," he ventured.

As he spoke, the man entered.

"Oh, here you are," Kildare said. "Did you get the river police started?"

The officer nodded.

"They're right on the trail. They will report by radio as fast as they get any news."

"Good." Kildare scribbled a number on a slip of paper. "I'm going to my apartment. Call me as fast as you get any news from them."

"Yes, sir," the other nodded.

Another figure popped in. It was the driver of the cab that had been waiting at pier twenty-seven.

"Say," he demanded, "who's going to pay me for this cab fare?"

"Just hang on a moment," Kildare said. "We'll go with you right away and I'll take care of the whole bill."

IT WAS nearly midnight when Hazard and Kildare reached the latter's apartment. They had dropped the first officer at the *Sussex* and he had promised to check up on the cask shipment immediately. Hazard dropped limply into a deep chair in the living room, took out a cigarette and lighted it.

Kildare went to his smoking stand. As he opened a cigar box and took out one of his long, slim cigars, he looked speculatively at his friend.

"I'm pretty dizzy about all of this," Hazard ventured.

"You mean about Wu Fang?"

Hazard nodded. "Yes. I can't picture him turning into an angel of mercy like this."

One of Kildare's rare, slow smiles spread across his face. "The fact of the matter is, Hazard," he said, "Wu Fang didn't do this unless he is getting something out of it."

Hazard stared. "You mean money?"

"No, no," Kildare chuckled. "I don't mean money. I mean that

Wu Fang is gaining something. I've been trying to figure out what it might be." He began walking up and down the room, puffing at his cigar.

"I would give a lot to know what's in those casks," he mused, reaching in his pocket, he took out the note that had been stuffed into Hazard's coat and read it again.

" 'Your friend until midnight Wu Fang.' Why, the yellow devil."

"At least," Hazard ventured, "we've got to admit that he kept his word."

"Yes," Kildare nodded, "I thought he would. Well—" His eyes turned to the clock on the mantel. "It's two minutes to twelve."

Hazard moved uneasily in his chair.

"Almost makes you feel as though you were due to be executed in two minutes, doesn't it?" he asked.

"Oh, I wouldn't say it was quite as bad as that. We'll have to be on guard a little bit more now, but don't let your nerves get you down, Hazard."

A gong sounded somewhere, far off in the night. Kildare glanced at the clock again. The gong struck on.

"H'm," he said, "either this clock is a minute slow or that big clock in the tower is a minute fast."

Bong, bong, bong, bong! The bell of the great clock off in the darkness clanged on. Nine, ten, eleven, twelve.

Kildare settled back in his chair and puffed at his cigar.

"Well," he said, "it's midnight." He smiled again.

"We don't seem to be in any particular danger so far as I can see. A lot has happened since we left the Press Club some three hours ago, but now everything is apparently peaceful again. We're safe enough here. Kind of a let-down, isn't it, from the fast action we've just been in? Nothing to do but sit, smoke, and wait for reports."

He wound one of his long legs around the other and then slowly unwound it again.

Hazard ran his hand nervously over his wavy hair. Kildare got up leisurely.

"I could do with a whiskey and soda," he ventured. "How about you?"

Hazard started to nod his head in agreement, but suddenly his whole body froze. His eyes stared into space and his hands tightened about the great arms of the chair.

"What was that?" he asked huskily, "that sound? Hear it? There it is again."

CHAPTER 6
THE GNAWING SOUND

KILDARE STIFFENED as he approached the little refrigerator in the sideboard. His apartment grew deathly still except for one sound, the sound to which Jerry Hazard had called his attention. It was a faint, rasping noise, something like the gnawing of a rat.

Hazard's blood chilled and his back seemed to have icy fingers playing up and down it. Suddenly, the sound ceased.

"Funny, isn't it?" Kildare asked; there was a bewildered look on his face. He glanced at the clock. "Do you know, that sound started just about the time the clock finished striking twelve?"

Hazard nodded silently.

Kildare walked over to the side of the room. An easy chair stood there with a stand beside it on which the phone rested.

"The sound came from over here," he went on.

Then once more they tensed.

Grind, grind, grind!

"That sounds an awful lot like a rat gnawing in a partition," Hazard whispered.

Kildare shook his head. "My dear man, rats don't gnaw partitions in buildings that are made of steel and concrete."

"Yes," Hazard nodded, "I suppose you're right. But it sounds like it just the same."

Grind, grind, grind! The noise went on.

Kildare moved away the chair, knelt down. He put his hand against the plaster of the wall and nodded slowly.

"I can feel the vibration of the grinding or whatever it is," he said. "It does sound like a rat gnawing. I'll have to admit that." Suddenly, he turned. "Maybe it's someone trying to grind through from the other side of the wall. I don't know how thick these partitions are."

"But you'd think they would know we'd hear them," Hazard protested.

"I don't know about that. The sound is muffled. If we were talking right along without much pause, we wouldn't be apt to hear it."

Suddenly he straightened.

"You know," he went on, "I don't know whether we hear it or feel it more. There's a vibration that carries through the floor. I can feel it through, my shoes."

Getting up, he went over to the desk at the opposite corner. He took out two automatics, inspected them to see that they were loaded and then handed one to Hazard.

"You'll probably need this before we get through. Might as well stick it in your pocket just in case." Then he took a flashlight out of the drawer. "It just seemed to me, that it might be well to bare a look in the apartment next to ours. I don't mind if it's occupied."

Gently he opened the door that led into the corridor. Even out there when they stopped and listened carefully, they could hear or feel that gnawing sound somewhere in the wall.

They approached the door of the next apartment. Kildare produced a bunch of keys, selected one out of the group and tried it in the lock. He worked with it gently, softly for a moment. Then the lock turned and he pushed the door in with his shoulder, holding the flashlight with his left hand and his gun with his right.

The beam spread out before them, lighting a vacant room. One sweep of the light showed them that their quest was useless.

"It's a cinch there's nobody here trying to get into my room," Kildare said softly. "Listen!"

The two men tensed again and waited. The room was perfectly still.

"That's funny," he decided. "We can hear it on our side of

the partition but not on this side. Maybe there's someone inside the partition!"

"You mean," Hazard ventured, "that there's a secret passage in the wall?"

Kildare hesitated, then shook his head. "No, that doesn't make sense. They don't build secret passages into these public apartment houses and still—"

He stopped again and nudged Hazard for silence. The sound was audible now. It was in the wall several inches above the floor.

"I'm not so sure about that secret passage being a crazy idea," Hazard whispered.

Kildare was tip-toeing over to the wall. Pressing his finger tips against the plaster he waited for a moment, shook his head. Finally he frowned.

"It isn't as loud in this room," he decided. "I can't feel the vibration as easily as in my own apartment."

The clanging of a bell startled them both. Kildare leaped to his feet

"Quick. That's my telephone."

He lunged for the door, raced out into the hall and dived into his own apartment. He jerked his head to Hazard

"Close the door," he ordered.

Then, he stopped short and stared at the phone. The bell was ringing loudly, but above it was another sound. It was that grinding, gnawing sound in the wall, right near the telephone. It was faster and much louder than before.

Kildare took another step toward the phone, reached out his hand; but Hazard clutched his other arm.

"Wait! It might be only a trap."

"We've got to take that chance," Kildare said

He lifted the phone from the hook, placed his handkerchief over the mouthpiece, took a long breath.

"Hello," he said, "this is Kildare speaking... Oh, yes. You have the address? That's fine. Will you give it to me, please?"

Bam!

UP TO this moment, the living room had been flooded with light, but now the lights suddenly went off as though someone had pulled a switch. The sudden darkness was accompanied by a crackling sound. Then came a cry—a sudden, low cry of alarm and fear.

Hazard groped frantically about in the darkness.

"Kildare," he gasped. "Are you all right? What happened?"

There was no answer. Just a sound of fumbling and then a bang as though something had crashed to the floor.

"Kildare," he called louder, "are you all right? What's happened?"

"Yes, I'm all right. I don't know what's happened. Wait. Hold everything."

His voice came from down near the floor. Then a beam of light slashed across the dark room in a fantastic pattern.

"Confound it," Kildare was saying, "I fumbled with the flashlight and it dropped to the floor. Wait! I've got to keep that phone call going. Hello, this is Kildare again... No, I don't think we were cut off. Everything is O.K. Go ahead…. What was that address?…. I see. Thank you very much."

The phone clicked as he hung up the receiver. The men faced each other in the dim glare of the flashlight.

"Did you get it?" Hazard demanded.

He saw the shadow of Kildare's head nod.

"Yes. Listen! That grinding sound has stopped. I haven't heard it since the lights went out."

"What was that cry?"

"I don't know," Kildare admitted. "I know the lights are out and we've got to get them on. That's the first thing. Wait, I've got to write down that address before I forget it."

He swung the flashlight to the phone pad on the table, scribbled on it. Then he opened the door and stepped out into the hall, which was plainly lighted.

"There's one sure thing," he said. "The lights didn't go out all over the house. It was just in my apartment. Here's the fuse box to my rooms. Let's see."

He dropped the cover.

"H'm, just as I expected. A fuse is blown. Well, a penny behind the fuse ought to do if the wires aren't crossed anywhere. If they are, it won't do much more than blow out the main fuse."

There was a jangle of coin. He unscrewed the fuse, pulled the switch, placed a penny in the back of the fuse socket, and screwed the burned-out fuse in again. Instantly the lights in his apartment blazed on. He smiled.

"I've got another idea. The apartments in this building are only about half filled. Let's go down to the floor below."

Even before he finished, he was running down the stairs. He strode to the door of the apartment directly below his and stopped short. A triumphant gleam came into his eyes.

"See," he said, "the person that was in here left in such a hurry he didn't even close the door."

He walked into the vacant apartment and slashed the darkness with his flashlight.

"See that!"

He pointed to a packing box on the floor, standing next to the wall. There was plaster dust all over the box and the floor.

"That's pretty good," he said. "Someone was standing on this box and grinding the concrete in the wall. I don't think he found what he was looking for. I think he—"

He turned abruptly, stepped out into the hall, ran up the stairs, and entered his own apartment. A very much baffled Jerry Hazard was following him.

"Now," Kildare said calmly as he closed the door, "I think we can have that whiskey and soda I mentioned. From the looks of you, Hazard, you certainly need it and I know I will appreciate it."

He produced bottles, glasses, and ice and proceeded with the mixing.

"For heaven's sake," Hazard exploded, "don't keep me in suspense. What's happened? I can't figure it out."

"I'm beginning to get the gist of this thing," Kildare said. "You remember I mentioned a little while ago that Wu Fang was going to get something out of this mystery? Tonight Hazard, I think we did him a big favor."

"I don't see how."

"I DON'T know," Kildare continued. "Why Wu Fang wants those five casks, but it's apparent that there's an opposing faction working against him. Those four men we locked up tonight are a part of that faction. Wu Fang had his agents on the *S. S. Sussex* and they learned what was going on. Instead of creating a lot of excitement by killing off these men he notified me about the intended murder and then had Mohra slip a note into your pocket advising us of the spies' escape. So we rush headlong to capture these European spies, as Wu Fang calls them—and as a matter of fact, I don't doubt but what they are exactly that. We captured them and locked them up. They are good for at least twenty-four hours, through that clever thought of yours, before they can even call in an attorney. I don't think that excuse of yours would hold in court, but apparently those foreigners believed it—and that's all that's necessary. So you see, we've really done Wu Fang a favor. Now he has clear sailing."

His eyes narrowed and he looked at the glowing end of his cigar thoughtfully.

"I've just got a hunch, though," he went on, "that Wu Fang doesn't know the address those casks were being shipped to— and he needs it. One of his agents must have overheard me tell the first officer to phone me tonight and as soon as he checked up on the address. This fellow downstairs was working his way into the walls to cut in on my phone line so he could listen to the conversation."

"Say, that sounds reasonable," Hazard agreed. "You remember how much faster that grinding sound went on after your phone rang?"

"Yes," nodded Kildare. "That's one of the things that gave me the idea."

"But what about the lights going out and that cry?" Hazard demanded. "Or was that due to the fact that—"

"I see you're getting it," Kildare smiled. "You see, this fellow was cutting into the wall and trying to get at our telephone wires. My theory is that he got hold of some wires and started tapping them with his telephone instrument."

His smile broadened.

"But the joke was on him," he continued with a chuckle. "Instead of tapping our telephone wires, he tapped our electric wires and unless I'm crazy, he got the surprise of his life. He shorted our lights and blew the fuse and at the same time, the thing startled him so that he cried out. Does that sound reasonable?"

"Perfectly. But what is the address you got from the first officer of The *Sussex?*"

Kildare frowned. "That's what has sort of got me stumped." He tore off the top sheet of the pad on the telephone desk and handed it to Hazard. "Know anything about that part of the country?" he asked.

"Post office box number five, Andover, New Jersey," Hazard read half aloud.

"I don't know much about that country," he said. "I was up there once, on an assignment. Had to interview a foreign ambassador of some kind who was spending the summer at one of the estates. I remember that it was beautiful country. Wild and mountainous."

"We'll be finding out before long, I imagine," Kildare said, "but I want to get some other things straightened first. We won't be going up on any vacation, however. You can rest assured that if Wu Fang learns of this address too, that wild country up there will be a great deal wilder and a lot less peaceful."

"I think," Hazard ventured, "I would just as soon take a chance of meeting Wu Fang and his agents in his Chinatown haunts. It's my guess that it's pretty lonesome country up there if any trouble, starts."

As he spoke, the telephone bell jangled again.

CHAPTER 7
THE MAN WITHOUT FEET

THIS TIME Kildare didn't bother to put his handkerchief over the mouthpiece. "Kildare speaking…. Yes, officer. You have a report? Fine! What is it?… I see. Very well. Will you do this? Call up and have a police boat pull alongside pier fifty-three as soon as possible. We'll be right down and get it…. Yes, that's right. Thanks."

He hung up and turned to Hazard.

"We're closing in," he said. "Now if Wu Fang doesn't beat us to it, I think we may be able to get those casks before he does."

"How?" demanded Hazard, all attention.

"The police boat," Kildare said, "followed the launch around the west end of Long Island out through the Narrows, past

THE CASE OF THE SCARLET FEATHER

Coney Island and Manhattan beach. The launch put in at a little cove about two miles beyond. The police boat is standing by and waiting for further orders. We're going there ourselves right now. This time we'll have guns and I imagine we'll use them."

As he spoke, Kildare grabbed his hat and coat. Hazard followed him out. When they arrived at the pier, they found the police boat waiting. It seemed that already the harbor police knew what was expected of them. They clambered aboard and the police boat moved off.

Kildare turned to the captain.

"Have you been in contact with the other P.B. that's standing by down off Long Island?" he asked.

"Yes," said the captain. "We just got a message from them. They asked how long they were supposed to stay down there I told them until we arrived."

"That's right," Kildare nodded.

The police boat was speeding down the Hudson River. It passed the Battery and the Statue of Liberty, ploughed out through the Narrows and turned east.

Once the captain asked curiously, "What's this all about?"

Kildare smiled and put him off with, "I don't know a great deal more about it than you do, captain. It's something in connection with the murder of Captain Atlee of The *S. S. Sussex*."

Nearly an hour passed. The police boat slowed her speed. The running lights were turned off as they nosed toward shore. Then a light blinked ahead of them, blinked and went out.

"There she is," the captain said, "out front. We'll pull alongside in a minute. She's heaved to right close to shore."

A few moments later they drew up alongside the other police boat and Kildare hopped aboard.

"I'm Kildare," he said in a low voice. "And this is Mr. Hazard. Now, may we have someone show us the way to the place where you have the launch man corralled?"

"Of course," the other captain said.

He detailed one of his men and they leaped ashore. It was pitch dark there under the overhanging trees. They had to feel their way along. The officer in front of Kildare seemed to know very well where he was going.

Suddenly, a shadow loomed from the side of the trail, a blurry figure. Hazard grabbed his automatic a little tighter and pulled it out of his pocket. Then he relaxed again as he heard the guide talking to the shadowy form.

A few whispered words that Hazard couldn't catch were exchanged and then the four of them moved on. They traveled perhaps fifty yards along the edge of the water, then stopped. A great, sleek-looking hulk showed through the darkness from the lighter area of the open water.

The officer who had met them on the trail pointed and whispered, "It's the cruiser. She looks pretty fast."

"That must be the one," Kildare whispered back.

"The launch that we trailed is tied up on the other side of the cruiser," the officer said. "Do you want to look it over?"

Kildare shook his head. "No. Where did the man go after be left it?"

"Follow me," the officer whispered, "and I'll show you."

They walked on stealthily, picking their way slowly so that they made little or no sound. After a short distance, the two officers stopped.

"Now," one of them hissed, "take a look through the branches. It's sort of a ramshackle summer cottage here. We trailed the man there and saw him go in."

"How could you do that?" Kildare demanded. "It's so dark I can hardly see the house."

"He was carrying a flashlight," the other answered. "He opened the door and then he closed it. We heard him slide a bolt from the inside."

Kildare nodded. "O.K. Come on. The only thing we've got to do is to be careful to take this place by surprise. We don't want to give them a hint of our presence here. I'll take the lead now, Hazard, you come with me."

SUDDENLY, HE stopped short. There was a sound beside them in the brush, the sound of someone moving. Hazard tensed and his gun hand clutched the butt of the automatic.

"That you, Monahan?" one of the officers asked.

"Yes," came the answer.

The first officer turned to Kildare with an explanation.

"This is my partner," he said. "He was watching the place while I went back."

"You are sure the fellow hasn't left by the back door?" Kildare demanded.

"Yes," said the other. "We haven't heard a sound since we came up here."

"Good. All right there's five of us. Hazard, you and I will take the front door. You men spread out, one at the back of the house and one at each end so that the fellow can't escape."

They moved out into the clearer space. Even at that, it was

He shuddered as he stared at the thing on the floor.

very dark, for the branches of trees that hadn't been cut to make way for the summer cottage overhung the clearing to a considerable extent.

Hazard and Kildare crept up on the porch. The boards creaked under them and with that, Kildare moved faster toward the door. He took hold of the knob and turned it and at the same time, he said in a low voice:

"Open ze door, Louis. Open quick!"

There was no answer. He rattled the knob now, rattled it insistently.

"Louis, you will open ze door," he said. "At once, Louis. Louis, are you there?"

Still no answer. Kildare frowned. "That's funny," he whispered.

"Yes," Hazard nodded. "What do you make of it?"

Kildare shrugged. "We're going to find out in a second," he hissed back. "I thought maybe we would get in easier this way."

He pounded with his knuckles on the door and tried to peer through the glass. A shade covered the opening inside, but it was apparently totally dark in there.

"Louis, what is wrong?" Kildare asked again. "Open ze door."

But the inside of the house was as still as death. Impatiently Kildare put his shoulder against the door, pushed. It gave way a little. He stepped back then and lunged, striking with his lean, hard shoulder low down, just above the knob. There was a crash and the door flew open before him.

He stepped inside and instantly his flashlight was on. He held it out in his left hand a foot and a half away from his body so that it would attract shots in that direction if there were any coming.

Then a voice from the other side of the cabin came to him. "Are you O.K.?"

For a split second, Kildare froze; then he stepped into the room.

"Yes, I'm all right. Where are you?"

Monahan's voice came back at him. "I'm here at the back door. It's open."

"Good Lord," gasped Kildare. "He got away then. I thought I told you—"

As he spoke, he was tearing through the interior of the building. His flashlight beam traveled ahead of him. It caught the form of Monahan silhouetted in the rear doorway and it caught something else, too—a splintered door hanging loosely from its hinges.

"I don't think he got away through this door," Monahan said. "Look here."

He pointed to the splintered door casing, to the broken lock. Then he produced a flashlight of his own to help in the examination.

"Lord, this is something," Kildare said. "This door has just recently been forced open. Look. The wood is new where it has been split apart from the rest. That's a crazy thing. What the deuce—"

"Yeh," said Monahan, "it looks like somebody broke in, but I'm sure of one thing. They couldn't have done it while we were watching the place because it's a cinch we would have heard the crash. There wasn't a sound after that guy came in the front door and locked it behind him. That's what struck me funny. He didn't even light a light. The door was broken open from the outside."

"Yes," said Kildare. "That's very apparent." He turned quickly. "Hazard, see if you can find a lamp. Let's get some light around here and don't mess up anything any more than you have to."

In the reflection of the two flashlights, Hazard turned and went out into the front room. It was plenty dark there, but he could see a little. He saw a white shaded lamp on a table and turned toward it. Suddenly, his toe kicked something. Something soft and yielding. Something that gave him a sudden start—as if he were kicking a bag of meal or a human body.

He stifled a gasp and darted back. Frantically, he fumbled in his pocket for matches and struck one, holding the flame so that he could see. But it was only for an instant. The match flared and then the breeze blowing from the front door to the back blew out the flame.

He stepped gingerly away from the object on the door that he had tripped over, but his feet came in contact with something else. Again it was something soft. He darted back once more, felt himself falling as his heel caught in something. He dropped his hands to catch himself.

As he went down, he heard a gurgling grunt. It was a horrible sound. A sound that came wet and thick. A sound that seemed half animal, half human. It froze his blood. Then his hand came in contact with the floor and with something warm and liquid and sticky.

He felt a mass of goo that gave him a sickly feeling at the pit of his stomach. His hands slipped in it and he was falling still farther.

He sat down with a thud on that same soft, yielding thing that he had first kicked with his shoe. He let out a shout. He couldn't help it now.

"Good Lord!" he heard Kildare exclaim as he came running

from the other room. The rays of the flashlight streamed into the room as Hazard struggled to his feet.

Then they stood, staring at a ghastly sight. Hazard's hands were red and dripping and he was shuddering unashamed as he stared at the thing on the floor.

KILDARE BENT over the ghastly figure when a match was struck and the kerosene lamp on the table glowed, shedding its light about the room.

Hazard came out of his sudden shock. Hastily wiping the blood from his hands on a dirty table cover, he too bent over the figure.

"I think," he breathed, "the poor fellow is still alive. He made a sound as I stumbled into him."

Kildare was making hasty examination. He nodded.

"He's barely alive," he said, "but there isn't any hope for him. Good Lord, look at the blood."

That last sentence was the best expression of the ghastly picture. On the floor lay parts of the body of a man. He was dark and swarthy. Blood oozed from his gaping mouth; what had been a tongue lolled from his lips, slit to ribbons.

His arms were stretched wide, but they ended in stubs at the wrists. Stubs where the hands had been neatly cut off. And the hands lay on the floor near the arms. Lay in pools of blood that had run from the wound.

His legs were stretched wide, and his feet, with the shoes still on, were severed like the hands. Severed at the ankles. The feet lay in two pools of blood where they had dropped from the legs.

Monahan breathed a prayer for mercy. The man without any feet moved weakly and then relaxed. Kildare felt of the heart action. Rolled back the eye lids.

"Dead," he said half aloud, and got up from the floor.

"That's got me stumped," he said turning to Monahan. "You're sure you didn't fall asleep while you were watching this cottage?"

Monahan shook his head vigorously.

"No, sir," he said stoutly. "I swear I had my eyes on the place every second. All I saw was this guy. I think it was him. About his height and all. I saw him open the front door and heard him slide the bolt. That's how close I was listening."

"The thing that bothers me," Kildare admitted, "is how they got at this fellow without you hearing it."

"They?" Monahan demanded. "Who?"

"Oh, I know who it was, or at least I've got a hunch," Kildare told him. "How long have you been watching this cottage, Monahan?"

Monahan thought for a moment glanced at a wrist watch on his arm. "I'd say it was about two hours," he guessed.

Kildare shook his head and his jaw clenched so that it gave his face a look of baffled anger.

"No one can tell me," he said, "that it took this man two hours to die from loss of blood with his arms and feet neatly severed at the wrists and ankles and his tongue slit to ribbons. It shouldn't have taken him more than ten minutes at the very most to bleed to death. And still you've been watching this place for two hours and you heard nothing."

The other two officers were coming in through the broken

down back door by now. Kildare turned and Monahan anticipated what he was about to say.

"Look, Gorsky," he said to the cop who had met them first
on the path, "you were with me all the time; we were watching
this place constantly. That's right isn't it?"

Gorsky added. "Yes, sir," he said to Kildare. "Monahan and
me was watchin' from the bushes and we saw this guy come
from the launch and go into the house and lock the door."

"I know," Kildare said almost savagely. "I've heard that story
at least four times. I believe you. But I wish you'd explain how
he was killed and when."

"As near as I can make it," Hazard guessed, "someone broke
down the back door of the shack before this bird came and
stayed to wait for him."

"Sure," smiled Kildare, "and when he came in they jumped
on him, struck him over the head." He bent down and felt of
the head of the dead man.

"Only," he said, rising again, "there isn't any bump on his
head to indicate that he was struck. Well, anyway, then they
caught him as he fell and while he was out cold the fiend cut
off his arms and feet. They did it very cleverly with a sharp knife
at the joints and there was no noise to that. And after that they
slit his tongue, then they left him to die. And we come along
two hours or more later and find the man is still alive and he
passes out while we're here. No, Hazard, there's something in
this that smells of fish to high heaven. It doesn't take a man in
that condition two hours to bleed to death."

He turned and glanced about the other parts of the room in the light of the lamp on the table.

"Have any of you seen anything of five small gallon casks?" he demanded.

Hazard shook his head. The officers did the same.

"I don't suppose they're here now," Kildare decided with a sort of sigh. "That would be expecting too much. But I would like to know if they've been here."

He picked up the lamp from the table and, holding it above his eye level, started on a tour of inspection.

"This place hasn't been lived in for some time," he ventured. "The floors are covered with dust. You can see—"

HE STOPPED short and stared across the main room. All eyes turned in the same direction. On the other side was a crude stone fireplace, reaching to the ceiling. The floor on the left was lifted up like a trap door.

Kildare strode over to it. Apparently, the trap door led to a cavity where firewood was stored beneath. But there was no firewood there now. Hazard reached Kildare's side and stared down into a semi-dark pit about two feet deep.

Kildare dropped suddenly to his knees, still holding the light a little above his head. He pointed to marks on the ground beneath.

"See there," he said. "See those five ring marks in the earth below?"

Hazard nodded. "They're gone, the things that made those rings."

"Yes," Kildare sighed. "Those five casks were hidden here.

And the man who was responsible for their safe keeping lies on the floor, dead. He's the one who picked up the casks as they were pitched from The *S.S. Sussex*."

"What was in those casks?" Monahan asked.

"Who knows," Kildare said with a shrug. "We've got to find that out."

Turning, he inspected the rest of the main room. He sniffed the air. Hazard had noticed something there too. Some strange odor that was not all unpleasant; but so far he hadn't thought much about it.

"Smell something funny?" he asked Kildare.

"Yes," Kildare said. "I was wondering what it might be. Smells sort of sweet. We ought to smell nothing much but a musty odor in this place that's been shut up for so long. But this has a very faint fragrance."

Hazard stiffened. Kildare was staring at him accusingly with the light above his head. Hazard's teeth clenched. He shook his head savagely and the muscles of his jaws bulged.

"No," he protested. "It couldn't be, Kildare. I know what you're thinking. She—she wouldn't do a—"

"Calm yourself, Jerry," Kildare said. "I haven't made any charges. But"—he sniffed again—"one can't help but let his imagination work a little. If I thought that she—" His teeth clamped shut and he turned.

"Let's have a look at the rest of the interior and see what we can find," he suggested.

With that he moved out into the back room, which was apparently used as a kitchen. He led the way with the lamp and the others followed. Nothing there. They returned to the large front room.

Against the inside partition a narrow staircase of unpainted wood ran up to a loft. Kildare climbed the stairs and peered about, then came down again almost instantly, shaking his head. "Nothing up there. And nothing has been there. The steps are covered with dust and there aren't any tracks in them."

He turned with the lamp just in time to see officer Monahan bend over and pick up something red off the floor. Before he reached him, the officer raised the object before his face.

He held in his hand a scarlet feather. A small feather that might have come out of any ordinary white foul and been dyed.

"This is what you smelled," he said. "Yes, it's this—"

As he said that last he held the feather very close to his nose, sniffed harder.

Kildare leaped then. With his free hand he caught Monahan's arm and pulled it down from his face. But the hand and arm dropped with horrible ease.

Monahan's eyes rolled for an instant. He reeled, clutching at thin air for support. Then suddenly, every vestige of rigidity left his body. Hazard leaped forward as he sagged, but he couldn't reach him in time to help.

With a thud, Monahan sagged to the floor, stretched out in a grotesque shape and lay still.

Kildare shouted.

"Quick. Hold this lamp."

Hazard caught the lamp and Kildare dropped beside the fallen officer. He straightened suddenly and stared from Monahan's formerly weather beaten face, from which most of the color had drained, to the small harmless looking feather that had fallen to the floor beside him.

For an instant Kildare poised there in thought. Then once more he slipped his hand inside Monahan's coat and tensed. Abruptly, he leaped to his feet.

"We've got to get him to a doctor. His heart is beating slower and slower. He's dying. Fading out on us. That confounded feather must have—"

He broke off short and picked up the feather in his own fingers. Stepped back while Hazard and the other two police officers lifted Monahan and carried him to the door.

The police officers were stouter than Hazard, and in moving Monahan through the door Hazard was just one too many. At that instant Kildare spoke in a low voice.

"Hazard. Wait here. Guess they won't need you. See this feather?" He held it up in plain view of the lamp. "It was found right by the door. Know what that means?"

HAZARD WAS trying to think clearly. But somehow, since the suggestion that the odor of fragrance in the cottage meant that Mohra had been there he had been unable to get his mind fully on anything else. He shook his head rather dumbly.

"It means," Kildare raced on, "that the victim had the scarlet, fragrant feather dragged under his nose just after he bolted the door. No man would come into a dark house like this, bolt the door and not light a light."

"But," Hazard countered, more to make Kildare think his own brain was working to than for any other reason, "if he was attacked and butchered right after he bolted the door, that would mean that he's been lying there on the floor bleeding to death for two hours. And you said yourself that that didn't make sense."

"Confound the impossible," Kildare snorted. "Nothing is impossible with Wu Fang on the job."

"You're sure then that this is Wu Fang's job?" Hazard asked.

"Positive," Kildare hurried on. "Remember another case when an inventor was killed! Wu Fang brought him back to his own house with his arms cut off and his tongue pulled out by the roots. But he was still alive and managed to tap out a message in code with his foot that your newsboy friend, Cappy, read. And that was what saved that day for us. But he didn't take a chance with this man. He cut off his feet too."

Kildare bent down over the bloody corpse of the swarthy launchman. He sniffed at the face, then got up again with a nod of satisfaction.

"That's it," he said. "I can smell the odor. But this scarlet feather—" he held it up in the light and stared at it—"is a ghastly combination of fear and death. That, perhaps, is the message that it's supposed to bring."

He took a business sized envelope from his inside coat pocket, extracted the letter, and placed the feather inside.

"We've got to hurry," he said. "I want to see what happens to Monahan."

Together, they half ran, half stumbled back to the police launch that had brought them. The first boat was already purring out of the cove. The captain of their P.B. jerked his head toward it.

"They're taking Monahan back as fast as they can. What happened?"

"Is he still alive?" Kildare asked.

"He seems dead enough except that there's the very slightest sign of a pulse."

As they raced on back toward New York, Kildare told the captain of the police boat what had happened. He was careful, however, not to shed much light on his reconstruction of the crime. At the docks he and Hazard took a cab.

"I must get back to the syndicate office," Hazard said. "Got to get a little work in before I get fired. You—you don't really think, Val, that Mohra was in on that ghastly thing, do you?" There was pleading in his voice.

Kildare shook his head.

"No," he confided. "It looked suspicious when I smelled that fragrance, but we know different now. I'll drop you off at your office if you like. I want to see you reach there safely."

Hazard grinned with relief.

"I'm glad you feel that way about Mohra," he said. "But you should worry about your own safety, old man. You know you're the one that Wu Fang is really after. Not me. He knows that without you, I'd be a terrible flop as a yellow peril tracker."

"You do your share," Kildare assured him with one of his slow smiles. "What are you going to write concerning this case we've been on?"

"I was just going to ask you," Hazard said.

"Anyone would think," chuckled Kildare, "that I was your boss."

"You seem to do pretty well at it," Hazard grinned back. "What's the answer? How much stuff do I put in the story? I've got to say something. A lot of people know already I'm in on this—the passengers on the boat and the news hounds that were covering the murder. I've got to turn something in."

"Let's work it this way," Kildare said. "Make out your report just as everything happened. Tell the murder story of Captain Atlee's death from an eye witness standpoint. Tell about the mystery of the kegs and the cruiser and the capture of the four suspects after they left the Sussex and the fact that they're in the jug. Everything except what Wu Fang is connected with. Put all of the blame on them. This last session we've just left— I'd forget that for this issue. Okay?"

"Okay," Hazard nodded.

The car was drawing up before the McNulty Newspaper Syndicate building. Kildare held Hazard a moment longer.

"About tomorrow noon we'll check up on that address of Box 5, Andover, New Jersey. If anything should happen to me between now and then, turn over all the dope to my federal friends."

Then he pushed Hazard out of the cab, and drove off into the night.

CHAPTER 8
THE SCARLET FEATHER

YOUNG CAPPY, Jerry Hazard's newsboy pal, was with the international reporter when he stepped in a cab about noon the next day and headed for the apartment of Val Kildare.

Cappy's eyes grew wider and wider as Hazard recounted his experiences of the night before; when he described the scarlet feather incident, he exploded with, "But gee, Jerry, that sounds like maybe some Indians are mixed up with it."

Hazard couldn't help laughing.

"I'm afraid you're due for a disappointment, Cappy, if you're expecting to find redskins in on this deal. There's a yellow skin behind a lot of it, but I don't think you'll find any Indians."

The cab stopped outside Kildare's apartment house and they went up to the federal man's apartment. Hazard knocked at the door; there was no response. He frowned and knocked again.

"That's funny," he said. "Kildare said he would see me here at this time."

Then he remembered Kildare's last words when he had left him hurriedly that morning. "If anything happens to me, turn over—all the dope to my federal friends."

Panic clutched him. Suppose something had happened to Kildare. Suppose Wu Fang—Cappy cut in on his thoughts.

"Gee, he isn't here."

Hazard shook his head.

"He doesn't seem to be, does he?" he said. "But let's hope that he's O.K."

He took hold of the door knob and turned it. The door was unlocked and opened quite easily. Hazard stepped in, followed by Cappy. Everything seemed in order. Hurriedly, he stepped across the big room toward the bedroom door, which was partly open.

His apprehensions were mounting. He was almost running as he thrust the door open wide. But everything appeared O.K. there. The bed had been slept in and was still unmade.

He breathed a sigh of relief.

"It looks as though he got around before we did and went out," he ventured. "In that case, he'll probably be back almost any time."

As he spoke, he heard footsteps in the hall. Then the apartment door burst open and Kildare strode in.

"Oh, good morning, Cappy," he said. "How are you, Jerry? Say, look here," he raced on. "I've discovered something this morning—a couple of things, in fact. Police headquarters called first to give a report on Monahan."

"Monahan," Hazard repeated. "Is he still alive?"

"Very much so," smiled Kildare. "It seems that red feather either isn't as deadly as we thought or else he has a particularly strong heart. Oh, they haven't let him go back on duty yet, but he's doing very nicely. This morning they were almost positive he was dead and then he rallied about two hours after that and his heart began beating again so that they could feel it. Now he's sitting up and eating."

He strode over to his humidor, took out one of his long cigars, and lighted it.

THE CASE OF THE SCARLET FEATHER

"I think I've figured out the explanation for one mystery," he said slowly.

Hazard's eyes lighted.

"You mean the mystery of the man who took two hours to bleed to death?"

"Exactly," Kildare nodded. "Look, here's the theory I've worked out. An agent of Wu Fang was standing behind the door when the launch man came in. He had this red feather in his hand. He waited until the man bolted the door, then he pressed the scarlet feather under his nose. The man's first instinct was to push it away—might have thought it was a cobweb or something.

"He made a move to brush it away and in doing so, knocked the feather out of the murderer's hand. The murderer caught him so that he wouldn't make any noise in falling. When this strange fragrance acted on the man's heart, Wu Fang's agent dragged him away from the door and proceeded to amputate his hands and feet and slit his tongue."

"You mean," demanded Hazard, "that Wu Fang's agent knew the feather wouldn't kill him?"

"He knew it might not kill him," said Kildare. "After he finished carving the boat man up, he went to find the scarlet feather, but he had a hunch the house was being watched and he didn't dare strike a light to look for it. He failed to find it and left."

"But," Hazard cut in, "I don't understand yet what kept this man from bleeding to death until we arrived two hours later."

Kildare smiled slowly. "I just told you that Monahan's heart began beating faster about two hours after the fragrant feather had knocked him out. In order for a person to bleed freely, he must have a good heart action to pump the blood out of him. That is why, for instance, in slaughtering animals, they give them a good bleeding before stopping the heart action completely. Take steers, for example. They sledge them in the head to knock them out and then cut their throats; and before they regain consciousness, they have bled to death. You see, there was no heart action sufficient to pump the blood out of the man's system fast enough. When his heart picked up, he began to bleed freely."

Hazard stared, admiration showing in his eyes.

"You certainly win the prize derby, Kildare, for figuring out that. You make it sound reasonable, but at the same time, I'll have to confess that I never heard of any drug that would stop the heart action in this way—and certainly not a scarlet feather."

Kildare smiled again, rather secretively this time.

"I THINK," he said, "you have heard something about this same scarlet feather before. You remember about two months ago, a Doctor Carver died, apparently from a heart attack, shortly after he had opened an ancient tomb in Egypt?"

Hazard nodded instantly. "Sure; it made a swell news story. The curse of the Pharaohs on him and all that sort of stuff."

"Yes." Kildare nodded. "Well, I just happened to think of it this morning. I don't know what brought it to my mind. I remember vaguely that one of the Sunday supplements ran a big story about the Pharaoh who had been buried in the tomb and his past history as recorded in tablets found by Carver and his assistant Powell, and it stuck in my mind that there was some mention of a very mysterious fragrant scarlet feather. I started out this morning in search of Powell, but I can't find the slightest trace of him. He has vanished from sight completely. So I went to the library and got out newspaper files a couple months old. The red feather was listed among the objects found in the tomb of Akmenatep. Also, I learned that the United States Government was in on the deal somehow through Powell."

"That is strange," Hazard admitted. "Then it was this same fragrant scarlet feather you have now?"

Kildare nodded, tapped his vest on the right side.

"I've got it right here in my inside vest pocket," he said in a low voice. "Our next move is a trip to the back country of New Jersey."

Cappy's eyes lighted eagerly. "Gee," he said, "are you going to take me too?"

Kildare smiled down at him.

"I'm afraid we can't make it this time, Cappy. I know you've been a lot of help to us before and we'll give you a chance again, but on this trip, we may be gone for a long time. You've got your paper-selling business to take care of, you know."

"Aw, gee," Cappy pleaded. "That can wait. I'll get along. Gee, something might turn up and you might need me. Besides, my Boy Scout troop is going up in the New Jersey mountains this summer to camp and I've been saving up to go with them. I've never been over there in the mountains and I want to see what it's like."

"If you're saving up for that camping trip, Cappy," Hazard

suggested, "you'll have to stay home and take care of your business."

Cappy hung his head. "Aw, gee," he said.

"You've got the gun I gave you, haven't you?" Kildare asked Hazard.

The news correspondent nodded.

"Hang on to it and keep it ready," Kildare advised. "We probably won't need it in the daylight, but darkness is only six or seven hours off and there's no telling where we'll be by then."

Cappy followed them out of the apartment house and Hazard flipped him a nickel.

"Sorry, kid," he said, "but the chief doesn't think you'd better go. You hop a rattler and get back to your stand. We'll cut you in when there's something real going on. I don't think this trip is going to amount to much anyway."

Cappy took the nickel and grinned. "All right, Jerry," he said. A cab was waiting at the curb and the two men stepped in.

"Through the Holland Tunnel," Kildare ordered. "Have you got a map of New Jersey?"

The driver's bullet head nodded on his thick neck.

"Yes, sir," he said. "I always keep one handy in hopes I might get a fare to Jersey."

As they rolled down toward the mouth of the Holland Tunnel, Kildare studied the map. Later, when they were in Jersey, he handed it back to the driver.

"Get on Route 6 and follow that to Netcong," he ordered. "Then follow thirty-one to Andover."

"Yes, sir."

THE CASE OF THE SCARLET FEATHER

The cab rolled through cities and towns and villages, and finally out into the open wooded country.

The afternoon was rather warm, and it got warmer as they drove. The window on the left was open only about an inch from the top. Kildare leaned forward and tried to lower it further. But as he struggled with the handle, it suddenly came off in his hand. He swore.

"These confounded taxi windows. We used to think sticking windows were a disease contracted only by railroad cars but it seems these old cabs have contracted the malady, too. Try the one on your side, Jerry."

The driver turned his head. "Sorry, sir," he said, "about them windows. I got a bum cab this morning. All the windows back there seem to stick. Anyway, I guess we'll soon be there."

"Thank heaven for that," Kildare said, mopping his brow with his handkerchief. "I haven't been so warm for a long time."

"It certainly is stuffy back here," Hazard agreed. "If we weren't traveling so fast, I'd open one of the doors and let some fresh air in."

"Better not do that," the driver advised. "I'd get in a lot of trouble if I lost one of these doors."

They were traveling on Route 31 now, through a lonely patch of country. For the last mile, there had been no dwelling on either side of the road. The cab passed through a railroad culvert and sped on.

The scenery began dancing in front of Hazard's eyes. He licked his lips.

"I feel," he started to say, "as though—"

The inside of the taxi didn't look natural. It was full of black specks as though the upholstery were made of a polka dot material. Kildare was there on the seat beside him, but he seemed to be merely a blurred figure in the afternoon light.

Hazard was fighting desperately to focus his eyes straight on his friend; he thought he saw him slump in the corner of the seat, but he couldn't be sure. Maybe he was sitting up and the strange, supernatural power that seemed to have hold of Hazard was making him see Kildare's body in a contorted position.

Leaning forward, he clutched the knob of the right-hand window. Frantically, he tried to open it. That was it. The stuffiness inside the cab was affecting them.

Then a feeling of horror rushed over him. His mind was becoming numb. He couldn't think clearly. But one thing stood out in his thoughts. It was the scarlet feather in Kildare's inside vest pocket. The fragrant poison from that red feather was doing the trick!

And yet, he couldn't smell any fragrant odor. Maybe his senses were already too dull.

In a wild effort to revive, he slapped himself as hard as he could in the face. For an instant, his head cleared a little, but his eyes danced all the more from the blow.

Then the cab lurched around a corner. He tried to see where they were going. He thought it was a dirt road, but he couldn't be sure.

Kildare didn't move. Hazard tried to call him, but his voice sounded far away and he realized that it must be coming in a mere whisper. He tried to shout to the driver—that thick-shouldered, ugly-looking bird who was crouched behind the wheel on the other side of the glass partition.

The driver turned and looked back at them, then drove all the faster. He felt a choking feeling now in his throat as though phantom hands were there pressing tighter and tighter.

One last thought came to him, came all too late. He leaned forward and reached for the door. If he could throw open that door and get some fresh air—His hand touched the door handle. Then suddenly, the floor of the cab was coming up at him—or he was floating down to it. He didn't know which and it didn't seem to matter.

Then lights went out completely and all consciousness left him.

CHAPTER 9
THE MAN WITH THE LIMP

EVERYTHING WAS confusion about Hazard as he regained consciousness. He looked up and saw men about him. There were long tubes curving down to his face and the men standing over him wore light blue uniforms.

He heard one of them say in a voice that seemed to travel from far away, "He's coming around now. I thought he would never make it."

Now his brain began to clear. He felt something on his face. It was a mask. He could just look over the top of it with his eyes. The mask covered his nose and mouth and it was into that mask that the rubber hoses led.

One of the men in the blue uniforms was saying, "That's right. Breathe deep. Fine! Now try it again. Don't try to talk or sit up until we tell you to."

Then he saw two other faces and those faces were familiar. On one side, Kildare was looking down at him gravely. On the other side was Cappy.

Hazard's eyes narrowed as he looked at the boy. He started to speak, and then remembered that he had the mask on his face and couldn't.

"Breathe deep," one of the men in blue said again.

Hazard had forgotten for the instant but he was breathing deeply now. The process went on, the process of bringing him back to full normalcy with the pul-motor.

His eyes traveled past the faces up to the sky. There were clouds up there and they were tinted with rosy hues. This must be sunset. If that were the case, at least two hours had passed since he had lapsed into unconsciousness.

Then the mask was lifted from his face. Those were New Jersey state troopers in the blue uniforms. One of them grinned down at him.

"How do you feel?" he asked.

"Not bad," Hazard replied. "Kind of woozy but—"

"Gee," Cappy cut in, "I was scared you were never coming back, Jerry."

Jerry Hazard looked at the boy fondly, then pretended to be angry.

"What I want to know, kid," he said, "is how you got out here!"

The boy grinned sheepishly. "Well, you see I got thinking about it after you and Mr. Kildare got in the taxi and I had sort of a hunch I had better go along. So when the taxi pulled away from the curb, I hopped on the back and rode inside the spare tire. I thought the cops at the Tunnel were going to stop me. Gee, I'm glad they didn't."

"It's a lucky thing for you that he came along," one of the troopers said. "You might have been flying around upstairs with a couple of wings on your shoulders if he hadn't."

"More likely I would have had a coal shovel in my hand," Jerry grinned. He stared suddenly at Cappy.

"Gee, kid, you've got a lump on the top of your head half as big as an egg. Who hit you?"

"The taxi driver," Cappy said. "You see, he didn't know I was there and when he began to throw you fellows out, I got hold of a rock and started after him from behind the car. Gee, I missed him by only a quarter of an inch. The rock sailed through the window and whizzed past his head. The guy turned then and caught me with a sock in the jaw. Gee, I didn't think I was ever going to stop sailing through the air. My head must have hit a rock because it knocked me out and when I came to, you and Mr. Kildare were lying here at the side of this dirt road and the cab and the driver were gone."

One of the troopers, a muscular chap with light hair, signaled to the other.

"Connell," he said, "get your note-book out and take down

the dope while I ask the questions." He turned to Hazard. "Now what was this all about? Have you any idea why the cab driver would pull such a stunt?"

Hazard hesitated and glanced at Kildare.

"I don't think either one of us knows much about it," Kildare said. "Apparently, the driver thought this was a good chance to get some easy money and—"

The trooper named Connell glanced at him quickly, suspicion in his eyes.

"That doesn't click," he said. "You fellows were gassed. I don't think a driver would go to all that trouble for a little money."

Kildare shrugged. "O.K., officer," he said. Then he flipped his federal badge into view.

"I'm sure there's nothing you can do about it, men," he went on. "I won't try to fool you with any funny yarn. Turn in whatever story you want to headquarters about our being gassed in the cab, but let it go at that. I would be just as well pleased if you would say it was robbery."

"O.K.," Connell nodded. "If that's the way you want it that's the way it will be. Can we take you somewhere?"

The light-haired trooper turned to Hazard.

"Do you feel O.K.?" he asked.

Hazard nodded. "A bit wobbly on my pins, but I'm coming back fast. I'll be all right."

"Then," suggested Connell, "suppose we drive you wherever you were going." He laid an affectionate hand on Cappy's shoulder. "It's a bright lad you've got here. The kid ran a mile and a half to the main road to phone us."

Cappy grinned. "Now you know, Jerry, where that nickel you gave me went," he said.

"We're headed for Andover," Kildare explained. "If you'll drop us off at the post office, well be very much obliged."

A FEW minutes later, they were standing before the Andover post office, which was a plain, frame structure. The troopers' car had moved away.

"I hope we're not too late," Kildare said. "Maybe it stays open for the evening mail like some of the post offices in other small towns."

He opened the door and stepped inside, followed by the other two. The place seemed empty. One entire wall was lined with post office boxes, with the exception of two windows. The larger one, marked "Packages", was just closing. Kildare stepped up before it quickly and saw a small, slender woman moving away. She turned her head, smiled pleasantly, and came back.

"Was there something you wanted?" she asked.

"Yes. I would like to speak to the post master."

The woman's smile broadened. "I'm sorry, but we have no post master in this office." And then, before Kildare could speak again, she added—"However, we do have a post mistress and I am she."

"You will do just as well," he agreed hurriedly. He displayed his badge and the post mistress' smile sobered slightly.

"We came," Kildare explained, "to learn the name and address of one of your box holders. It's box five."

The woman's mouth set in a firm, straight line and she ceased to smile.

"I am sorry," she said, "but I am not permitted to give out the name and address of that box holder."

"You mean," Kildare demanded, "that you can't even give it to a federal agent? You see, I'm working for the federal government the same as you are."

"I am sorry, but I have special orders from the post office department to give the name and address of that box holder to no one."

Kildare hesitated a moment, then one of his slow smiles spread across his lean, weather-beaten face.

"I think," he said, "you would be very successful in secret service work. Have you ever considered taking it up?"

The post mistress shook her head. "I am quite well satisfied here. But thank you for the compliment—if it was a compliment."

"It was, and thank you for doing all you could. We'll try not to cause any trouble."

He stepped back and the post mistress closed the window. Through the glass they could see her sorting the evening mail. Townspeople began drifting in now. Kildare stepped to the opposite wall and jerked his head to Hazard.

"Don't take your eyes off box five," he ordered. "If someone gets mail out of it, follow him. I'll be back as soon as I can."

He went out and Hazard and Cappy took up their quiet vigil watching that innocent-looking box with a number five painted in gold on the glass.

Minutes passed. Then Kildare re-entered. He glanced quickly at Hazard, who shook his head.

"Nobody's been in yet."

Kildare nodded. "We'll wait," he said.

But in less than a half hour, the post mistress came out from behind the row of lock boxes.

"I'm sorry," she said, "but you will have to leave. I am locking up for the night."

They filed out and she followed, locking the door behind her. Kildare strode down the street with Hazard and Cappy on either side of him.

"What do we do now?" Hazard asked.

Kildare shrugged. "Just stick around. If it takes until Doomsday, we've got to wait here until we see who takes mail out of box five." He turned as he spoke. "The post mistress has just gone around the corner," he said. "I think we can go back safely now. We'll wait in my car."

"Your car?"

Kildare smiled. "I just rented one. It's standing near the post office. We just passed it."

THEY WALKED back to the car, a small sedan. Kildare dropped in behind the wheel, started the engine, and drove it slowly up in front of the post office. Here he slowed almost to a stop, glancing over his shoulder into the office window as he did so.

"There," he decided. "We can wait right here. The street lamps shed a little light inside. If anyone goes to box five, we can see them from here."

"But gee," Cappy protested, "the post mistress just locked the door."

"I know," Kildare nodded, "but I've got a hunch. Another thing—do you know why we were gassed in that taxi?"

Hazard shook his head. "I've been wondering, but haven't had a chance to ask you."

"That was one of Wu Fang's agents driving the cab," Kildare said. "Don't ask me for proof. The trick would have worked out very nicely—for him—if Cappy hadn't been along. As a matter of fact, it didn't go so badly. When I regained consciousness, which was about an hour before you, my coat and vest were open."

"You mean the scarlet feather?" Hazard demanded quickly.

Kildare nodded. "That's it. It was gone. I think you also know by now that your gun is gone. Mine is. But we can't waste time worrying about that."

Pitch darkness fell over the village and still they waited. Waited until Jerry Hazard became too impatient to keep still any longer.

"Honestly," he exploded, "I can't see any sense waiting here. I think Cappy's right. It's—"

Kildare nudged him; the government man was looking into the rear view mirror over the windshield.

"A car has just pulled up behind us," he said tensely. "Turn your back toward the door on the street side. There, that will hide me better so that they won't be able to see that I'm watching."

"Gee," Cappy said from the back seat. "He's getting out and going into the post office. Look! He's an old guy that walks with a cane and he limps."

Kildare was nodding his head. "Sssh! I think that's our man."

The man that they were watching was short and wiry. In the light of the street lamp, he seemed to be past middle age. As Cappy had stated, he walked with a cane and limped, but at that, he moved with a quick step like one who had been accustomed to doing so in the past.

Without the slightest hesitation, he walked past the post office entrance, turned sharply up a vacant lot that bordered the building. Here his small, limping form melted into the darkness.

"Well," Hazard breathed, "that's that. For once, you guessed wrong, Kildare."

Kildare smiled.

"No, I don't think so. Wait and see. Or, I mean to say, don't see. Keep your back to the sidewalk so that I can look past you. That's it."

Two minutes passed. Then Kildare breathed triumphantly. "There, I knew I was right. He's in the post office now."

"What?" Hazard gasped.

"Don't turn around. I can see someone moving around inside and the only way he could have gotten in is through the back door."

Hazard felt Kildare tense.

"He's opening box five now," he whispered. "Now he's taking out letters and closing the door. He's going to the rear of the building again. Watch now. In about a minute or so, you'll see him come around through the vacant lot."

The prediction was correct. In a little over a minute, the man came limping back through the vacant lot. As he passed the car, Hazard felt Kildare move closer to the window. He saw him stare; the street light must be falling on that man's face now. Then he let out a surprised exclamation.

"Good Lord, it's—"

He stopped short. Hazard, who still had his back to the sidewalk, heard the footsteps of the limping man. He heard him open the door of the car behind them, heard the door slam. Then the engine purred, and the car drove off up the road.

Instantly, Kildare followed.

CHAPTER 10
THE FRIGHTENED MASTIFFS

"WELL, I'LL be doggoned," Hazard exploded. "You ought to qualify as a fortune teller, Kildare."

"Not as a fortune teller," Kildare smiled. "Just as a good guesser. I got a hunch when I was talking to the post mistress that the holder of box five is connected with the government. That means he might be given a key to the post office so he could get his mail when nobody was around."

"I still don't see how you figured it out. But about this man with the limp. You spoke as if you know him."

Kildare switched off his lights as he followed the car ahead off on a side road.

"I do," he nodded. "He's old 'Rocky' Madden. He used to be a mighty good federal agent, then he got pretty badly shot up in one leg. That was just about the time I started working for the Government. He's up here on some special job and you can make up your mind that if they put Rocky Madden in charge, it's something darn important."

The car ahead was moving faster up the winding road, Kildare's sedan bumping and jolting along behind it. The country was thick and wooded after a mile or so, Kildare shook his head.

"They certainly picked a lonely spot," he admitted. "Nobody would ever think of anything important coming off up here. Nothing, that is, except a good hunting trip."

The lights of Madden's car vanished around a sharp turn. A few moments later Kildare took the same turn; suddenly, he switched on his lights and jammed on the brakes.

The car they were trailing was parked crosswise of the road. There wasn't a chance of getting around it. A small, dark form sprang from the brush at the left and a voice that was electric with authority cracked out in the black night.

"Stop and reach!"

Kildare was stopping as fast as he could. Jerry Hazard grew tense and his arms crawled up over his head, but Kildare only laughed. Keeping his hands on the wheel, he answered that challenge calmly.

"I'd know your voice, Rocky Madden," he said, "if I heard it in the Gobi Desert."

A flashlight beam cut across from the side of the car and turned on Kildare's face. Then a low exclamation escaped the lips of the other.

"Kildare, Val Kildare! What are you doing, following me?"

Kildare chuckled again. "It looks as if I'm showing myself

up as a darn fool. How did you know I was trailing you? I had my headlights turned off."

Rocky Madden grinned. "I always make a practice of coming up that last stretch of road and rounding the turn fast. Then I shut off the motor and listen. You were making as much noise coming up as a thrashing machine. This is a private road, you know. Didn't you see the sign?"

"I had my lights off," Kildare said. "I didn't notice any sign. There seems to be a lot of mystery around here."

"Are these others with you?" Rocky Madden demanded.

Kildare introduced them. "We've been trying to find out who holds box five," he explained.

"Well," said Madden, "you haven't found out yet."

"No, but that's what we're here for. Listen, here's the lay of the land."

He raced on, touching the highlights of what had happened concerning the five casks, the scarlet feather, and the murder. Madden hesitated, then shook his head.

"I can't let you in," he said, "without special permission. For one thing, it would be too dangerous for you. We've got a bunch of mastiffs up here guarding the place and I'd have to get permission from my chief to lock them up first; they're the most ferocious beasts I've ever seen."

"Mastiffs, eh? What are you hiding out here, Madden? It must be something mighty important."

Madden nodded. "I'll say it is. Stay where you are. I'll go talk to the chief, then come back and let you know."

"O.K." Kildare said.

THE CASE OF THE SCARLET FEATHER

THEY WAITED almost twenty minutes before Madden returned. "It's O.K.," he announced. "Powell says to bring you on up. He's very anxious to discuss things over with you."

"Powell?" gasped Kildare. "Do you mean Dr. Carver's assistant?"

"Sure. Do you know him?"

"No, but I just saw his name this morning. It was in the report of the discovery of the tomb of—"

"Sssh! Better wait until you get up there."

Kildare glanced about in the darkness. "Do you suspect someone is watching us?"

"I don't know," Madden said, "but things look funny. Mighty funny. Come on. Follow me in your car."

Madden returned to his car and started on ahead. Now with his lights turned on, Kildare found it easier to follow. They passed through a great hole in the forest where low, overhanging trees gave it the appearance of a cave.

"Gee," Cappy breathed, "what a swell lay-out for a murder."

The car ahead stopped. Madden got out, opened a high wire gate. He drove through and stopped on the other side; then he motioned Kildare to come on. When they had passed, he closed the gate behind them.

"Stay in your car," he said, "and watch out for the dogs. I'll tell you when to get out."

"Does this wire fence enclose the whole estate?" Kildare asked.

"Yes. There's about a hundred and fifty acres."

As the lights of the moving cars circled around, Kildare saw

97

a great, gorgeous structure looming through the trees. It was a mansion of Italian design, a large country villa with a formal pool in front that was crumbling a little at the edges and grown up with weeds and cat tails. As they swung around the drive, they could see that the building itself was crumbling in places; patches had peeled off the walls here and there.

Madden's car drew up before the house and was greeted with a deep, bellowing roar. It was the roar of an animal. It grew to a savage bark and then tapered off to a whine—a whine of fear.

From somewhere near the corner of the house came other barks and whines, ending on a note of fear. Then a growl started. Started and stopped abruptly, as though it were choked off.

Madden got out of his car, slammed the door and shouted, "Shut up."

Then he stepped to their sedan and opened the door.

"I think its O.K.," he said. "If the dogs come for you, I'll try to drive them off."

"I hope you are successful," Kildare answered drily.

Another deep-throated howl shook the night. Then there were whines that sounded like the whines of big, panic-stricken puppies.

Hazard felt a chill passing over him. He climbed out of the car on Madden's side and opened the door for Cappy.

"I wish you hadn't come, kid," he said. "This doesn't look so good."

"Well, gee," Cappy told him. "I'm not afraid."

Silently, the four mounted the steps of the villa; no lights were visible in the house. A dark object came slinking noiselessly across the porch floor. Madden turned his flashlight on it instantly, revealing a giant mastiff crouched on all fours.

"Back, King," he snapped. "These men are friends."

The dog stopped, his eyes glowing in the light of the torch. Madden took another step forward, then hesitated. The dog started coming on again, his belly almost touching the floor. He was not creeping up on them to spring, but was crawling like a licked puppy, a puppy with broken spirit. And he was trembling; he whined now and trembled still more.

"Come here, King, old man," Madden said more softly. "What's the matter?"

The dog slunk up to him, shaking with fear. He licked the toe of his right shoe and whined.

Hazard felt the cold sweat pouring out of his forehead.

"It looks," Kildare ventured, "as though King knows something we don't know."

"Yes," nodded Madden. He spoke to King again. "Back, boy," he said, reaching down and patting his head.

Then he led the others toward the door. There was no sign of protest from that great, cringing mastiff dog. He was just plunging one hand into his pocket for the key, when the door opened. A pale light shone out, silhouetting a young man of average stature who was standing in the open doorway.

"Come in," he said quickly.

They filed in and he closed the door behind them. Madden then performed the ceremony of introduction.

"Gentlemen, this is Mr. Powell, my chief."

"I'm mighty glad you've come," Powell said. "Do you know anything about dogs, Kildare?"

"A little," Kildare admitted.

"Come into the library, won't you?" Powell asked.

He was a quick-spoken, alert man and he moved rather nervously. He led them across the entrance hall, which was of spacious size, to a room opening off it.

HAZARD STARED about in the light of several lamps. Once, perhaps, massive Renaissance furniture had filled this room, but it had apparently been removed and in its place were scantier pieces, enough for comfort, but not enough to take away the strange, lonesome feeling which he had of a mansion that has been stripped of its beautiful decorations. A small fire glowed in a fireplace; the walls were lined from floor to ceiling with empty book cases.

Hazard jumped as a sound came from a shadowy corner beside the fireplace. It was another whine. Turning quickly, he stared in that direction. A great mastiff crawled across the floor. There was no brave gleam of challenge in its eyes, only supplication and fear. Hazard saw Powell bite his lip.

"Caesar," he barked, "what's the matter with you? A few hours ago you would have howled your head off if those men came in. And now look at you. Aren't you ashamed of yourself? Get back in your corner."

The dog whined again and slumped back to the blanket from which he had come.

Kildare took the cigar from his coat pocket, surveyed it ruefully. It was broken toward the end. Carefully, he took out his knife and cut it off below the broken point, then he produced his lighter and began puffing.

"Confound those dogs," Powell complained. "They give me the creeps. I can't imagine what would make them act this way."

Kildare didn't wait to be asked to sit down. He dropped into a heavily padded chair, slumped into his characteristic position and wound one long leg around the other. Puffing thoughtfully at his cigar, he glanced at the great window. Hazard glanced in that direction, too, as he lighted a cigarette with fingers that were none too steady. Heavy drapes were pulled tight in front of the window. Kildare seemed satisfied with that.

"You know," he said, "animals sense when things go wrong much sooner than human beings do."

Powell turned an agonized face to him. "But what can be wrong? We've got this whole estate enclosed with a heavy wire fence. Besides, I doubt anyone knows we're here."

Kildare hesitated, glanced at the whining dog again, then turned to Madden.

"When do you go down after the mail, Rocky?"

"Twice a day. About eight o'clock in the morning and at night."

"Do you go to the post office in the morning, too?"

Madden shook his head. "No. The post mistress helps sort the mail when the seven o'clock train comes in. Then she goes back home for breakfast. She takes the mail for box five with her and I get it at her home."

Kildare nodded slowly. "Then at night, you always get it after the post office is closed?"

"Yes."

"Somebody," Kildare said, "trailed you this morning."

Madden shook his head stubbornly. "They couldn't have. I stopped around that sharp turn on the way back and listened for a long time. There was an airplane overhead, but there were no cars following me up the road."

Kildare muttered under his breath, "The devil! The yellow devil!"

Powell jerked around and stared at him. "What do you mean?"

"Simply this," Kildare said. "Wu Fang or one of his agents was in that plane. He knew ahead of time that he could not find out who was the owner of box five by asking the post mistress, so he took other means. He used his head, too."

"You mean," gasped Powell, "that Wu Fang knows where we are and what we're doing?"

Kildare nodded.

"Wu Fang and his agents and all of his ghastly methods for ferreting out secrets are here right now in the woods surrounding this house. If you don't believe it, look at your dogs. They know."

CHAPTER 11
CURSE OF THE PHARAOH

POWELL MADE a snorting sound of disgust. Hazard stared at him puzzled, then suddenly he realized just how the inventor felt. The same feeling seized him—a desire to stand up and yell out defiantly:

THE CASE OF THE SCARLET FEATHER

"Bring on Wu Fang and all his agents! I'll fight them until every drop of blood in my body is gone." And then to sink down, shaking with the knowledge that this defiance was only a frantic effort at self-assurance—a pathetically hopeless effort.

Here they were in this great, crumbling Italian villa, at least two miles from any other living inhabitant. It was pitch dark outside. The one element that had been counted on to guard the house and grounds from trespassers, the mastiffs, were cringing hulks of dog flesh. Afraid of something that they, in their dumbness could not explain. Deathly frightened by a menace to which their masters did not know the full answer.

"How many are there of you here, Powell?" Kildare asked.

"Three," Powell answered hollowly. "But look here, Kildare, this is going a bit too far." He mopped his brow with a handkerchief. "It looks to me as though you're trying to frighten us out of our wits with this talk about dogs sensing something that—"

"Wait," Kildare cut in quite calmly. "I know you only by reputation as an archaeologist and precious little about you as that except that you found the tomb of Akmenatep with Carver. But I know Rocky Madden. And I know that Rocky Madden isn't to be frightened by talk of dogs sensing something that humans don't understand. I doubt very much if anything ever frightened Madden in his life. Speak for yourself when you mention fear."

Rocky Madden was studying the tip of a glowing cigarette he had just lighted.

Powell glanced at the floor for an instant, then he lifted his eyes squarely to Kildare. And his eyes didn't waver.

"I've let myself go too far," he confided. "It's this infernal isolation. Why, I haven't been out of this place since I was sent here by the government. It seems to have come to a climax tonight, with the dogs going queer—and then Madden comes with the tale you told him of Wu Fang and—"

He straightened with an effort. "You don't know. If—"

Kildare waited but Powell didn't go on. After an uncomfortably long pause he said:

"Well, Powell, you were going to say—"

The muscles of Powell's face were tense. "I—I—"

Kildare moved with utmost calm. Anything to quiet this sudden bundle of nerves named Powell. His voice came softly.

"You said there are three of you here at this place. Who's the third party?"

Powell seemed momentarily relieved by that question.

"The third party is the cook."

Kildare's one leg that was hung over the other unwrapped itself and he leaned forward.

"Chinese?"

Before Powell could answer, Madden spoke.

"No."

"Thank heaven for that," Kildare sighed and settled back in his chair.

"This fellow's name is Justin," Madden explained. "He's a full-fledged American and a mighty good cook. He's done work for the Government before. I can swear that he's okay."

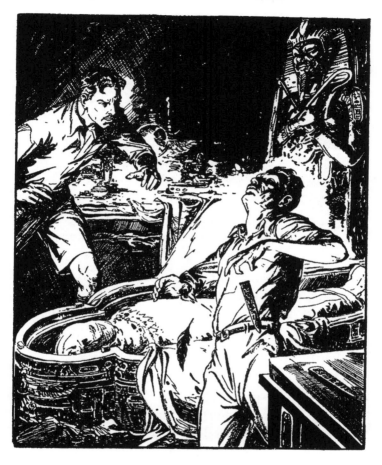

"He sniffled at the scarlet feather, then suddenly slumped lifeless."

Kildare nodded, signifying that that matter was settled. He relaxed still deeper into the comfortable chair, as if he were getting set for a long talk.

105

"Powell," he began, "you were with Carver on that tomb expedition. You went through some harrowing experiences, didn't you?"

"Yes. There wasn't anything pleasant about some of them."

"And you came through with your self-respect preserved?" Powell's eyes lighted in angry surprise. "What do you mean?"

"Simply this. You didn't go to pieces like you have tonight. Come. Buck up, man. Suppose you tell us about that scarlet feather. At the moment I'm particularly interested in it."

Powell hesitated for a short moment. Then he said, "You're wrong about *that* feather, Kildare. There were two of them. I've never told the whole story to anyone, except one person. That's why I'm here now."

"That person was a high United States Government official?"

"There aren't many higher," Powell confided in a low voice. "But—" His teeth clenched and he shifted nervously in his chair. "Confound it, I may as well tell you the whole story from beginning to end.

"Carver and I were working together when we discovered the tomb of Akmenatep. It was noon of a hot day, after a week of digging, that we found the great stone door. We got it moved aside and tested the interior for dangerous gas that might have formed during the centuries. After we were sure it was safe, we went in. We were both excited because it was obvious the tomb had been intact since it was first sealed shut, several thousand years ago.

"There was the usual sort of stuff. Bracelets. Chairs. Household goods. Tables of ivory and gold. Priceless objects for the museums. It was a thrilling experience, I can tell you."

HE WAS engrossed in his story now and forgetful of the dangers that had tightened his nerves a few moments before.

"There was a golden chariot heavily carved and a pair of small gold horses hitched before it. There were gorgeous vessels of food, sealed tight for the spirits of the departed dead king. I could go on telling you about them for days. And of course the biggest thrill of all was knowing that we, Carver and I, were the first to enter that tomb for—well, at a rough guess—four thousand years. That's a long time, Kildare, as we reckon time."

"Yes," Kildare nodded. "It is."

Powell frowned.

"But there were two things very strange about that tomb. One was the odor. There was an earthy, musty odor, of course; but there was something else that seemed to cut through that and top it off, as you might say. It was pleasant, like that of a strange, unknown flower.

"The other strange thing was the fact that there were two sarcophagi. Usually a tomb held one sarcophagus unless the king and queen were buried in the same place. But—" He took a long breath as though to fortify himself—"There was no queen. In fact, there was no sign that any mummy had ever been in that sarcophagus."

"It was empty when you opened it?" Hazard demanded.

"Exactly."

Kildare showed a little more interest than before. "And the

other sarcophagus," he suggested. "That, of course, had the mummy of Akmenatep?"

"Yes. The empty gold sarcophagus was the most interesting of the two for it was almost completely covered with Egyptian hieroglyphics. But the sarcophagus containing the mummy of Akmenatep carried merely a short inscription—the name of the king."

Powell paused and a hush came over the half bare room, broken only by the whimpering of the great mastiff beside the fireplace.

Out in the night one of the other dogs let go a blood-curdling howl that echoed and re-echoed through the great house. Then it died away in that strange, unexplainable whining. The mastiff beside the fireplace took up the cry.

Powell turned jerkily to the big beast. "Be still," he cracked.

The dog whimpered twice, stuck his nose deep down between his powerful paws and looked reproachfully at his master.

"What did the inscriptions say on the empty casket?" Kildare urged.

"Er—oh, yes," Powell started. "But perhaps I'd better keep the story to just the way things happened.

"After Carver and I had studied the inscriptions on the empty casket without much success, we each started a thorough search of the smaller objects in the tomb.

"But it was he who happened upon what turned out to be the most interesting and the most horrible as well.

"I was looking over some gold trinkets that lay on a little

bench of finely wrought gold. I heard him say, 'Powell, look here. This is odd.' I turned and started toward him.

"I saw he was holding a small gold dagger shield. But instead of a dagger it held a feather. A scarlet feather. As he pulled it out he asked, 'Have you smelled that fragrant odor ever since we entered?' I answered that I had."

The mastiff whimpered again. Hazard stirred uneasily and glanced at the beast. And at his glance, the dog slunk his head down and fell silent once more.

"I remembered then that when we first came in, I had noticed those two objects—which I took to be knives in shields—lying on a black carved stand at the foot of the empty casket. It struck me there should have been a sign above them reading 'Take One.' They were that handy, you see. I had started to pick one up, then the inscriptions on the empty sarcophagus diverted my attention.

"Apparently, while I was snooping about one side of the tomb, Carver had come back to this little stand. Perhaps he had felt the same way about them; I'll never know that. Anyway, there he was, holding that feather he had just drawn from the gold shield. And he said, 'Powell, that fragrant odor is much stronger since I took this feather from the case'."

Powell grew rigid in his chair.

"Then," he said, "it happened. Carver lifted the feather to his nostrils. I saw him sniff. I saw his face light up as though he made a discovery. Then to my astonishment, he suddenly slumped back as if all the life had gone out of him. I ran forward, tried to catch him, but he fell before I could get hold of him.

"When the doctor of the expedition reached him a few minutes later, he was dead."

HAZARD STIFFENED in his chair as a mastiff yelped from somewhere behind the house. Kildare turned his head quickly and stopped to listen. The beast beside the fireplace stood up; and for the first time since they had entered the room they heard the animal growl. It was a sound that was not nice to hear. Deep and guttural and blood-curdling.

"That dog," Kildare said. "The one that yelped. Something has happened to him."

Powell got up and walked across the room toward a closed door that led to the back part of the house. Then he stopped short as though listening and waiting.

Hazard heard those footsteps, too. They were padding along at a half-running gait beyond the door. Powell raised his voice and at the same moment that his cry echoed through the vaulted library, the door burst open and a middle aged man in shirt sleeves rushed in.

He stopped short, stared about in surprise.

"Oh," he said, "I beg your pardon, Mr. Powell. I didn't know you had guests, but—"

"Go on, Justin," Powell ordered. "What is it?"

"One of the dogs, sir. It was Duke that we keep chained outside the kitchen door. He's been whining considerably tonight—like the others. I heard him yelp just now as though he was hurt or frightened. I rushed out to him and—he's dead."

"Dead?" Powell groaned, then started for the doorway in which Justin was standing. Instantly Kildare was on his feet.

"Stop," he barked. "Don't go out there. You of all people must stay in the safest place!"

Powell stopped short and stared uncertainly. Kildare was already beside him to make sure that he didn't go farther. He turned to the cook.

"I think," he said, "you left the back door open. Or perhaps the draft I feel is my imagination."

A guilty look crossed the cook's face. "I—I came in such a—"

Kildare leaped past him through the dining room. Passing the buffet he snatched a carving knife, then charged on, through the kitchen door.

Cappy and Hazard reached the kitchen in time to hear the back door slam shut. Then Kildare was shouting a warning.

"Keep back unless you've got a club."

Hazard grabbed the boy and pulled him back.

"Get a knife," he ordered, "a fork, a club—anything you can find in the dining room. Find the switch and light a light."

Kildare's eyes were glued to the crack under the door; they switched from there to the edge of the kitchen. With his left hand he flung open a cupboard door. At the same time, he yelled.

"Get ready. It's coming your way. Stamp on it with your heel. For the love of heaven don't let it—"

He broke off. Hazard was poised, one foot raised. The short hair on the back of his spine was standing up straight. He was sure of that. And he felt as though he were frozen to the spot.

Just then Cappy flashed up.

"Here, Jerry," he exclaimed, "I got a couple of heavy candle sticks. What is it?"

"I don't know," Hazard told him.

Madden, Justin and Powell were crowding behind him, making it hard for him to move if it became necessary.

"Get back, all of you," he cracked. "Go into the library and close the door. Madden, keep Powell there."

He didn't turn to see if his orders were obeyed. He heard sounds of scuffling feet and took for granted that the three had retreated.

He was trying to see past the partly open door, beyond which he could hear Kildare thrashing around.

He heard Kildare grunt. Then a door slammed, and the federal man came into plain sight, dashing across the kitchen floor. Something that was small—ghastly small—was traveling with lightning speed ahead of him.

Kildare struck with the carving knife again and again. But the tiny wriggling thing seemed to know where he was aiming, and dodged successfully each time.

Suddenly Cappy, who was standing beside Hazard, dashed into the kitchen. The lad was traveling fast, too, the heavy metal candle stick raised in his hand.

Kildare tried to move him back. But Cappy didn't pay any attention. The wriggling thing swerved straight for him. And at that moment the lad slipped. He was falling and the wriggling thing was directly under him.

Thump! Thump! Thump!

Cappy's club was hitting furiously. Then the lad landed with a crash and lay still.

CHAPTER 12
THE EMPTY SARCOPHAGUS

HAZARD LEAPED forward with a cry of alarm. "Cappy! Cappy, are you all right?"

The figure of the boy moved, raising up one of his hands.

"Gee," he said, "Look! I got him."

"Thank heaven for that," Kildare panted. "I never saw anything run faster in my life."

"Look," said Cappy. "It's still moving."

The three stared down at a tiny thing wriggling there on the floor. It was a scant four inches in length. Hazard shuddered.

"Why, that thing," he said, "is small enough to crawl through the tiniest crack in a door or a window."

The thing was slimmer than a lead pencil and a dull brown in color, a brown that exactly matched the color of the kitchen floor. If it hadn't been moving, it wouldn't have been noticed, so nearly did it match the color of the floor. There was a dent in its back about an inch behind its head where Cappy's candle stick had cut it almost in two. But parts on either end were still wiggling convulsively like the tail of a dead snake.

Kildare bent down and poked it with the carving knife.

"I wondered," he said, "how it could move so swiftly. I had to keep it on the go to keep track of it. The minute it stopped moving, it turned the color of whatever it was on, like a chameleon. See, it's got legs, little tiny legs that are so slim you can hardly see them."

"And look at that head," Hazard ejaculated.

He pointed toward it, keeping his fingers well out of reach. The head was that of a miniature adder. The jaws were opening as the forward part of the body jerked convulsively back and forth, back and forth. There were two needle-like fangs, each a quarter of an inch long. The eyes of the little creature gleamed hideously.

Kildare touched the head with the end of his knife and in spite of the fact that the body was severed in two parts, the head whirled and struck with such speed that the naked eye couldn't follow it.

"That," Kildare said, "is the fiercest little beast I have ever seen in my life. I dare say it's the prize of Wu Fang's collection of hybrids. It has the ability of a chameleon to match whatever color it's against. And those fangs are sharp enough to penetrate a tough skin."

Madden's voice came from the dining room.

"What's happened? Are you all right?"

"Yes," Kildare shouted. "We've caught the thing. Come in, if you like, and have a look at it."

Rocky Madden, Justin, and Powell entered the kitchen, stared down at the creature.

"Good Lord!" breathed Powell. "Why, that isn't any bigger than a fair-sized fish worm."

"It's a lot more deadly, though," Kildare countered. "I can assure you of that."

"Do you think," Justin asked, "this is what killed the dog?"
Kildare hesitated. "I am not positive. You see, when a poisonous snake strikes, it injects all the poison from its poison sac, and several hours are required to generate more poison. I have a hunch that something else killed the dog."

"But look here," Justin inquired, "if it wasn't this reptile that killed the dog, how did it get in the kitchen?"

"That's easily answered," Kildare admitted. "Knowing Wu Fang as I do, I would say the dog was killed because he was in the way, and then you played right into the yellow devil's hands. When you heard the dog yelp, you ran out to see what had happened and, in your haste, left the kitchen door open. This little beast"—he pointed to the thing that was still wriggling in its death agony on the floor—"was sent in here to get you."

Justin shuddered visibly.

"But why," he demanded, "would they want to get me? I'm just the cook."

Kildare nodded. "Apparently, so far as Wu Fang is concerned, you're just another watch dog to get out of the way."

They heard Powell's breath come in a quick gasp of horror.

"Shall we return to the library?" Kildare suggested. "We have a few more things to talk over."

Powell nodded.

"Yes, let's get that over with. I—I have a feeling that I would like to have someone else know my secret before the night is over. You see, something happened today that nobody else knows about yet."

KILDARE PICKED up the wriggling form of the serpent

on the end of the carving knife and carried it to the library where he intended tossing it into the fireplace. The great mastiff suddenly leaped to his feet. He tensed, ready for a spring, and an angry growl filled the room. It was a growl of angry ferocity. He wasn't whimpering now. The hair along his great back bristled and his long, powerful teeth were bared in a snarl.

"Back, Caesar!" Powell yelled in alarm. "Back, boy."

But the dog didn't obey. He came a step farther, his eyes fixed on the little, dangling body on the knife blade. Kildare lunged quickly toward the fireplace, gave the knife a hasty whirl toward the glowing coals. But he wasn't fast enough.

The two-hundred pound mastiff pounced; his head tossed in the air and his teeth snapped together with a clicking sound that wasn't nice to hear. He had caught the reptile in mid-air and as his teeth vised upon it, he snarled furiously.

The next second a sharp yelp of pain echoed through the room. The dog swayed and then as suddenly as the horrible little scene had begun, it was over and the dog's great body dropped with a thud to the floor.

Kildare shook his head. "I'm sorry, Powell. I tried my best to toss the thing into the fire, but the dog caught it in midair."

Powell was tight-lipped and white-faced. He gave a short, nervous nod.

"Yes," he said. "I know. I saw it."

"Nevertheless," Kildare went on, "it proves one thing. This wasn't the snake that killed the other dog." He turned to the cook. "It was sent in to get you, Justin, but—"

He lifted the reptile on the end of his knife from where the dog's body had dropped it and tossed it into the coals. They heard the little worm-like thing sizzle and then flames came up and shrouded it.

"I also think," he continued, "I have the answer to the frightened dogs."

"I thought," ventured Madden, "you explained that before."

"I did," Kildare said. "But I believe now I was wrong. I now believe the dogs' fright is mainly due to an odor that they have smelled ever since Wu Fang and his agents have arrived." He turned to Hazard. "You remember, Jerry, my theory of how Wu Fang controls his beasts with odors? One odor is something repugnant to all animals; the other odor attracts them—at least, it attracts these poisonous beasts of his. It's the repugnant odor that the dogs have smelled and it's that that has caused them to act the way they have—"

The howl of another dog out in the night came to them—a howl that ended in a whimpering whine of fear.

"And still does," Kildare finished. He turned to Powell. "I believe we had just reached the point in your story where the doctor found that Carver had died from smelling the feather. Let's all sit down and try to compose ourselves again. I'm very anxious to hear the rest of your story."

They sat down. Kildare fished out another broken cigar from his pocket, clipped it off like he had done with the other, lighted it, and settled back in the same easy chair he had occupied before. Hazard lighted a cigarette.

The muscles of Powell's face were working, but he managed

to say, "Yes, yes, I remember." But he didn't seem to remember. He bit his lip and looked down at the floor.

"I believe," Kildare prompted, "you were going to tell us something about the inscription on the empty sarcophagus."

Powell showed relief as he nodded.

"Oh, yes. I had studied Egyptian hieroglyphics to some extent, but it took the assistance of one of the best men in that line to work out this message; and it was a very strange tale that empty sarcophagus told.

"It seems that Akmenatep was a ruthless king and, I suspect, a bit insane. He ruled his subjects with an iron hand and death by the fragrant feather was the only punishment used during his rule. It seemed, too, that killing by the scarlet feather became a religious rite; the feathers were really considered to be sacred. It seems horrible, doesn't it, to think that something sacred should be used for the purpose of execution?"

Kildare nodded. "And about the poison," he ventured. "Of course these feathers weren't naturally poisonous."

"Of course not," Powell agreed. "The message went on to state that the empty sarcophagus was to receive the body of the first unbeliever who disturbed the tomb and smelled the sacred scarlet feather."

"You said," Kildare reminded him, "that there were two feathers. You have both of them?"

Powell shook his head. "No. Some time after Carver's death, the feather which killed him was stolen."

"And the shield? Was that stolen, too?"

"No. I have both shields and one feather." He lowered his

voice almost to a whisper. "I have them here. I was deeply grieved, of course, to lose Carver. After his death, an idea began to grow on me. You see, archaeology is a hobby with me; my profession is actually chemistry. During the war I was a government chemist and developed poisonous gases for use in France. So when I saw Carver killed my first thought was—what a valuable weapon this drug would be in case of war. I took the matter up with—well, with the high government official that I mentioned a little while ago. We talked it over and it was decided that I should set up a small laboratory and isolate myself so as to work on this thing in perfect safety.

"You see, my idea was first to find out what this poison was that Akmenatep used on the feather to produce instant heart failure, and then to expand it until we could put it in the form of a gas. About three weeks ago, I learned the nature of the poison and informed my chief in Washington of the fact. It's a very rare poison made from an insect called the *teclito* that at one time was quite common in Egypt. It is fairly rare now. The poison derived from it is called *agretol*. It isn't even commonly known to chemists in this country, although I found a small quantity of it here being used in the treatment of a rare heart malady. Through investigation, we learned there was a quantity of it stored in Vienna—five bottles. It had been obtained some years ago by a certain eminent Viennese physician in the belief that, combined with another fluid, it would be a cure for cancer. I've been working with the small quantity available in this country. This very day I completed my experiment."

He lowered his voice to a husky whisper. "You are the first

ones to hear about the final success of my experiments. The gas will be the most ghastly menace ever used in warfare. I had no idea of its terrific killing power until my experiments were completed. But I know now and it's almost unbelievable."

He leaned forward in his chair, tense with the importance of the information that he held.

"This *agretol* poison is very rare. But it is terrifically strong, strong enough so that in the formula I have discovered, ten drops of *agretol* combined with the proper quantity of gas would be enough to kill the inhabitants of a city of a hundred thousand."

A HUSH of horror fell over the room as Powell finished. Kildare's voice sounded a little husky when he broke the silence.

"And the five bottles of this poison have been shipped from Vienna, Powell?" he asked.

"Yes. They each contained something like a quart of the poison. That's why my nerves have been so shattered since I learned they were stolen. Perhaps you don't realize it, but there's enough *agretol* in those five bottles to kill every living person in the world instantly if it were properly combined with the gas I mentioned."

"Jove!" Kildare breathed. "No wonder Wu Fang is trying to get this thing." He stared with narrowed eyes at the glowing end of his cigar. "I wonder how much Wu Fang really knows about it—and how much is just guess work."

He stopped short. Nobody could answer that question. His gray eyes lifted suddenly from his glowing cigar butt and he turned quickly to Powell.

"How about those five casks? I am assuming, of course, that the bottles were inside the casks."

Powell nodded. "Your assumption is correct, Kildare. That was the idea of my chief. He had a government man who happened to be in Vienna pick up the poison and pack each bottle in a cask with straw around it. Then the casks were tightly sealed and addressed to my post office box."

"That was where a mistake was made," Kildare cut in savagely. "This ring of European spies happened to stumble on the fact that these five casks were being shipped out of the country. There was so much secrecy about them that they decided to investigate."

"But how," demanded Powell, "did Wu Fang get hold of this information?"

"Heaven only knows," Kildare said, shaking his head, "how Wu Fang gets in on a lot of things. But he does. Apparently, Wu Fang's agents are everywhere. It's obvious that every spy ring in the world is watched by his agents. Yes, Powell, that was a grave mistake. We wouldn't be in the jam we're in now if those five bottles had been shipped as medicine to some big hospital in New York from that hospital in Vienna. Do you see? It's like seeing a man running headlong down a street in the night. You suspect that he's fleeing from something—the same rule holds here."

Kildare stopped and stared at his cigar butt again.

"I'm a little curious," he went on, "to know how you stumbled on to the poison formula. Chemical analysis?"

Powell shook his head. "I tried to analyze it, but was left

pretty much at sea because, as I have told you, *agretol* is a very rare poison. As a matter of fact, I had never heard of it myself and I've done a lot of work in Egypt. I got a hint from some of the inscriptions on the sarcophagus. You see, most of the inscriptions are in ordinary hieroglyphics. But there is a group at the foot that is very unusual. When I came here to work, I had the empty sarcophagus moved up here."

"You mean?" Hazard demanded, "that you have it here in this place!"

Powell nodded. "It's in the next room, which I use for a laboratory. Would you like to see it?"

Kildare unwound his legs and got up.

"By all means," he said. "And I want to look over your laboratory, too."

As Powell lead the way to the opposite side of the room, Kildare stepped to the heavy drapes that shrouded the window and adjusted them to make sure they were tight. Then he followed the others.

Hazard frowned in perplexity as he watched Powell walk to the wall. There was no door—only the great mass of empty book cases towering to the ceiling. Powell lowered his voice.

"You see," he said, "the room I chose for my laboratory is sort of a hidden chamber. It was apparently built for a place where the owner could slip away and be alone if he wished without fear of being bothered."

As he spoke, Powell stepped to one of the strips of carved wood that bordered a block of book cases, touched a button. There was a gentle click; then he took hold of the case and it moved out into the room, revealing a small entrance. He entered first and snapped on the light. When all were inside, he turned and pulled the book case back in place.

THE ROOM was small, not much more than ten or twelve feet square. Along one side was a lead-covered work bench with three tiers of shelves ranged above it. Bottles of different shapes and sizes stood on the shelves and chemical apparatus on the work bench.

But that wasn't what gripped Hazard's attention. It was the other side of the room, which was occupied by a table from the tomb of Akmenatep. Beside it, a gorgeous gold box, big as a coffin, gleamed. It was standing on end.

Powell pointed at it.

"There it is," he said.

Kildare shook his head.

"It has always been a wonder to me how anybody could read that stuff."

"It's quite simple," Powell said, "when you understand it. That is, until you run up against a snag such as I did with the hieroglyphics on the foot here. If you will give me a hand, I'll tip the box down and show you what led me to the discovery of the poison."

The sarcophagus was heavy, but with the three of them working, it wasn't a hard job to tip it over and lay it down on its bottom on the floor. Then Powell moved to the foot of it and pointed to the hieroglyphics there.

"You see," he said, "the predominating figure is the queer-looking insect. It so happens that is quite a good reproduction of the *teclito*. Now, if you will help me tip it up on end again, we will have more room and I'll show you how the history of Akmenatep reads on the cover."

The sarcophagus was tipped up on its end again so that it stood upright. Taking a position before its closed cover, Powell began pointing out the various hieroglyphics and explaining them. That finished, he turned to the laboratory work bench, where he unlocked a drawer and pulled out two small gold shields. One was empty. From the other, the quill of a feather extended about an inch.

"There," he said, "are the two shields and the one feather. I keep them well hidden and I think it would be safer if we don't handle them too much."

So saying, he replaced the two shields in the drawer and locked it again.

Hazard was glancing about the small laboratory, apparently with the same idea that Kildare had, for the federal man asked the question which was uppermost in his mind.

"Where do you get your outside light and ventilation?"

Powell pointed to the end of the room, high up toward the vaulted ceiling.

"There's a window up there. You can see it's heavily draped. I don't think there's a chance in the world of anyone ever climbing up there from the outside because there's a straight drop of about fifteen feet from it to the ground. I keep the drape just as a precaution when I work at night. This experiment is so confounded important."

"I should think so," Kildare nodded. "How about trying something for me, Cappy?"

"Sure," said Cappy. "You tell me just what you want and I'll try my best at it."

Kildare lifted the boy to the end of the lead-covered laboratory bench.

"Now," he whispered, "climb up on my shoulders. I'll try to balance you, then take you over to the window. When I give the signal, pull the drapes back as quickly as you can."

"Yes, sir," Cappy said.

He climbed to Kildare's shoulders, balanced there for a moment. Then Kildare, holding the boy by the legs, moved carefully toward the draped window. Cappy lifted his hands to the curtains and took hold of them.

"Now!" Kildare snapped.

The boy gave a sudden jerk and the heavy drapes flew apart.

There was a sudden cry of alarm and Cappy jerked back so quickly that he lost his balance.

Kildare tried to catch him, but the boy was falling over backwards. Hazard rushed up, grabbed him just as he fell.

"Cappy!" he exclaimed. "What is it? Are you all right?"

The boy's face was ashen white. His lips were moving, but he couldn't seem to speak for a second. Kildare bent down over him.

"You saw something, Cappy, didn't you?" he asked tensely.

The boy gave a nod of agreement. Then words began to come from his colorless lips.

"Yes—yes," he gasped, trying to catch his breath. "I—I guess it surprised me. I didn't expect to see anything. It was there looking in the window."

Kildare nodded. "Yes, I saw something, too, but I couldn't tell what it was. I was looking up and couldn't get a good view of it; besides the light reflected on the window pane. What did it look like to you, Cappy?"

The boy's lips were quivering again.

"Gee, Mr. Kildare," he blurted out, "please don't think I'm a coward. I—it scared me so. I don't know what it was. It couldn't have been what I saw. It looked like—"Then the boy shook his head again, savagely this time. "No," he said stubbornly, "it couldn't have been that, Mr. Kildare."

"What?" Kildare demanded. "Jove, Cappy, can't you tell us?"

"Gee," Cappy said, "but you'll laugh at me. You'll think I'm crazy. It was a face close to the glass. It was the face of—of a baby!"

CHAPTER 13
MURDER IN THE NIGHT

KILDARE WHIRLED to face Powell. "Have you got any lights on the outside of this building?" he snapped.

Powell was just standing there, staring dumbly at the window, over which the drapes had fallen back in place. Kildare's quick words seemed to snap him out of the horror that filled the whole laboratory.

"No, no, we haven't," he stammered.

"Good heavens!"

"We—we never expected anything like this to happen," Powell said defensively. "We thought—"

"Yes, yes, I know," Kildare cut in quickly. He started for the door of the laboratory, but after two steps he stopped and turned back.

"No," he said, "that wouldn't do any good."

"I've got some flashlights," Madden offered hurriedly, "if that will help any."

"I'm afraid not," Kildare said. "We haven't a Chinaman's chance of seeing anything with a flashlight." He broke off short with a grunt. "H'm," he said, "that's a good one. A Chinaman's chance. It looks as though we haven't got a chance against a Chinaman."

"I know you couldn't find it, Mr. Kildare," Cappy said. "It's run away by now. I'm sure of it."

"Yes," Kildare nodded. "You're right, Cappy. We couldn't find it and while we were traipsing around in the darkness, we would probably find a lot of things that we didn't expect. No, I don't think it would do any good to go out there. Anyhow, it will be a lot safer for us to stay—" He turned and faced the boy. "Now tell me, Cappy, just exactly what you saw."

The lad was growing calmer now and was getting better control of himself.

"You raised me up to the window and I pulled back the curtains, Mr. Kildare," he said. "Then I saw it. There was a face there, right close to the window and gee, it scared me awful. I never saw anything like it in my life."

"Did you see anything but the face?" Kildare asked.

127

"Well, I couldn't see much," Cappy said. "I guess that was because I was too scared. I think, though, there were some arms holding the face."

Kildare frowned.

"You mean someone below was holding a face up to the window?"

The boy shook his head. "No. I don't think it was like that. It was more like the arms were attached to the body that the face was on, but I couldn't see the body. That is, I don't remember much about it. There were arms up on either side of the face. It looked like they were hanging to something on the side of the wall."

"Why," Powell cut in, "the boy's crazy. There isn't a thing out there that anything but a leech could cling to."

Cappy turned quickly. "Well, then, it must have been a leech, Mr. Powell, because I saw it hanging there and I don't think it was standing on a ladder."

"Did anybody else see what Cappy saw?" Kildare asked.

The others shook their heads.

"I saw something move," Hazard said.

"So did I," Kildare agreed, "but that was all. I couldn't distinguish what it was. How big was the head, Cappy?"

"Well, gee," Cappy said, "it was just about like I said. It looked like a baby's head and a baby's face, although it was kind of wrinkled and shriveled up around the eyes and mouth. As soon as I pulled back the curtains it dropped from the window. I guess that was when I dropped too. I was so scared and wanted to get away from it so bad that I lost my balance."

Kildare turned to Madden.

"How many guns and flash lights have you got here, Rocky?"

"I've one," Madden answered, "and Powell and Justin have one apiece."

"O.K. I would like to make a suggestion. We want to play this thing as safely as we can. That means that we've got to shut up shop, go to bed, and turn off all the lights."

"Good Lord!" Hazard exploded. "You don't expect us to get any sleep tonight, do you?"

"No, but we've got to make it look as though we're figuring on it."

"But look here," Powell demanded. "With the lights off, we'll be in darkness and then we won't be able—"

"You mean we won't be able to see," Kildare said. "That's just why I want the lights off so that we will be able to see. When we get the lights off, we'll pull the drapes back from every window in the place. When our eyes get accustomed to the dark, you'll find that we can see much better from inside out than they can from outside in unless they've got cat's eyes— which I wouldn't doubt a bit."

Powell hesitated, but Kildare grasped his arm.

"Come on, we'll begin by turning the lights off here. Madden, you go and collect the guns and flashlights. Come on, Cappy. Up on my shoulder again." The boy obeyed instantly without hesitation. "Now out into the library, all the rest of you. Powell, you turn out the light and Cappy and I will be right along."

AS THEY filed out of the laboratory, one by one, Hazard was reminded of a jury leaving a murder case. Only this time, it was the other way round. A murder would be committed against them. He was trying his best to figure out just what was going to happen. The whole situation was horrible, ghastly. Strange things looming in the night, beasts and reptiles—and now this baby face at the window. He had to confess that Cappy had a stout heart for there he was again, up on Kildare's shoulders at the same window.

"There you are," Kildare was saying. "See anything?"

"No," said Cappy, "not this time. I didn't think I would."

"You've got the stuff it takes, Cappy," Kildare commended as he lowered the boy and followed him out of the secret room into the library.

"Thanks, sir, but gee, I was awful scared first time."

"We all get scared at times. The trick is not to let the other fellow know it."

Rocky Madden was coming in from the hall, carrying two automatics, a police revolver, and three flashlights. He laid them on a table in the center of the library together with two boxes of ammunition.

"There," he said, "that's the works, Kildare."

Kildare nodded. "Thanks. Now, let's see. Powell, where have you been sleeping?"

"On the second floor. For the most part, we have been occupying the rear section using this library for a living room and the bedrooms above it. But I can assure you there will be no sleep tonight for me."

"You will have plenty of company in your waking hours," Kildare assured him. "Cappy, how do you feel? Pretty sleepy?"

"No, sir. Gee, I don't believe I could go to sleep tonight, Mr. Kildare."

"You ought to try," Kildare advised him. "You need sleep, you know."

"Yes, sir," Cappy nodded, "but I would just as soon go right on living if it's all the same to you."

Kildare smiled. "I think, Cappy, you and Powell had better take the same room. What have you up there for beds, Powell?"

"For myself," Powell replied, "I prefer an army cot—a comfortable one with springs and mattress. There's another one in the hall; we can make it up if you would like to have the boy sleep in my room."

Kildare nodded. "Fine. Will you go up then? I wouldn't draw any shades. Just turn on the light and prepare for bed as you usually do."

Powell stared in astonishment.

"For heaven's sake, Kildare," he protested, "what are you thinking of? Do you mean we are supposed to go up there and expose ourselves in the light to the woods beyond. There's trees, man, right outside the windows."

"Fine. That's just what I want." He lowered his voice almost to a whisper. "I want those who are watching from outside to think that we suspect nothing. I want them to see you and Cappy going to bed as if nothing is happening. It may throw them off their guard and at any rate, I want them to know where you and the boy are spending the night."

Powell shrugged. "Very well. If that's the way you want it.

But I'll be perfectly frank with you and confess it gives me the creeps."

"Keep your window closed and locked," Kildare advised.

"What good do you think that will do?" Powell countered, "if somebody is planted outside in one of those trees and takes a shot at us?"

One of Kildare's slow smiles spread across his face.

"My dear fellow," he said, "apparently, you don't know much about Wu Fang. Wu Fang doesn't shoot people. I wish he did, instead of the way he does kill them off."

"Very well," Powell said reluctantly, turning toward the hall door. "I hope you know what you're talking about."

Hazard saw Cappy glance significantly at him. There was a worried look on the boy's face; Hazard forced a grin that he didn't feel at all to reassure the youngster before he vanished into the great, dimly-lighted hall. Kildare turned to the others.

"Justin, where do you sleep?"

"I have the second room from Powell's."

"Is there anything off these rooms? I mean, any roofs or verandas?"

Madden shook his head. "No, that's why we picked 'em."

"And your room, Madden?"

"I have the one between Justin and Powell."

Kildare nodded. "All right, Justin, you can turn in."

"Will—will it be all right if I lock my door?"

"Yes," Kildare agreed. "Lock everything that you can. Lock and bolt yourself in and try to get some sleep."

"Try to," said Justin as he started down the hall. "That's a good one."

They heard the cook's footsteps dying away as he walked across the stone paving of the hall to the stairs. Kildare picked up one of the automatics and examined it carefully. He slipped it into his right hand pocket and put a flashlight into the left one.

"I think," he said, "we're ready to turn out the lights. The three of us are going to keep watch for a little time."

"I can't think of anything I'd rather do in this place," Hazard admitted.

"It's all right with me," Rocky Madden nodded. "You don't care if I take the revolver, do you? That's my favorite."

"Not at all," said Kildare as he switched off the lights. "Hazard, you take the other automatic and stick it in your pocket."

HAZARD FELT a bit more secure when he got that automatic in his right hand pocket and a flashlight in his left. It made him feel as though he had a chance now. Not much of a chance, he admitted to himself, but more than before. The room was pitch black, but a few moments later he saw a glimmer of pale light at one end. Kildare had reached the windows and was pulling back the heavy drapes.

"See anything?" he whispered.

"No," Kildare hissed. "No use wasting any time here now. I want to make a tour of the house and make sure that everything is locked up. You lead the way, Madden."

Hazard followed as the two led on through the great mansion. They passed into the dining room, switched off the light that had been left in the kitchen. They went carefully over the entire first floor.

Now and then, a howl came out of the night, a howl that always seemed to end in that fearful winning of a great dog in mortal terror. They had completed the circuit and had returned to the great hall when Kildare suddenly clutched Hazard's arm in a signal for silence.

"I thought I heard something," he hissed.

"What?" Hazard gasped.

"I don't know. It sounded like a scratching on a window pane."

"Perhaps," said Hazard, "it was somebody upstairs. They're just turning in for the night, you know."

"Yes. Stay here and listen."

Kildare stepped away from them and vanished in the darkness. They could hear his footsteps crunching ever so lightly on the stone paving as he went toward the front door. He came back a moment later.

"The door's locked. Let's go upstairs and have a look around up there."

They followed him up the dark stairs to the upper hall.

"You lead the way," Kildare whispered to Hazard. "I want to take a look at all the rooms—except Justin's and Powell's. They've probably locked themselves in by now."

Try as they might to muffle their footsteps, they seemed to ring and echo through the great, dark spaces. They covered room after room. Each time, Kildare crept to the window, peered

134

from the side of it, tested the lock to make sure it was fastened securely.

"Now," he whispered, "let me get this straight, Rocky. This closed door is the room where Powell and Cappy are spending the night. Right?"

"Right," Madden whispered

Kildare crept down the hall. "And this door next, is open. Is this your room?"

"Yes," Madden said.

Kildare reached the room, turned into it. Then he stopped stock still and grasped Hazard's arm so tightly that his fingers dug painfully into the flesh. At the same time he moved his gun hand; it came up with lightning speed. At that instant Hazard became aware of what had evidently alarmed the federal man—a slight draft of fresh air was blowing across his face! He saw something move outside the window. Then as suddenly as he had grabbed it, Kildare let go of his arm and leaped across the room.

Hazard was only one jump behind him. Madden couldn't move so quickly because of his lameness. Kildare stood there an instant, staring out. Then he took hold of the window, which was open perhaps two or three inches, and raised the lower sash noiselessly. With extreme caution, he peered out and down into the night.

Hazard froze with suspense. He was trying his best to see, but he couldn't make out anything except blurred, dark shadows.

A moment later, Kildare turned inside and lowered the sash

with the same noiseless skill that he had exercised in opening it. He felt for the lock and made the window fast.

"I wish I knew," he muttered, "what that was. I would have sworn I saw something move on the sill. Did you leave the window open, Madden?"

Madden hesitated. "I'm afraid," he said, "that I did. But Great Scott, Kildare, a fellow can't live in a hermetically sealed building."

"Of course not," said Kildare. "On the other hand, there are worse ways of dying than by suffocation. Well, everything is locked up now, I guess. Maybe my nerves are getting a little tight and making me see things. It might have been a movement of one of the tree branches outside. If not, there's no telling what may be in this room now—but I would rather not turn on the light here. I think we'll take a chance and say it was my imagination."

They went out into the hall and Kildare nodded to the next door, which was closed.

"That's where Justin is spending the night, isn't it?" he asked.

"Yes," Madden answered.

"All right. Now, let's go down into the library and—"

He stopped short. An angry snarl rent the night, to end in a quick and terror-stricken yelp. Kildare breathed a sigh.

"Another one of the poor brutes," he whispered. "We can be ready for almost anything at any time now. Let's go downstairs to the library. The big library window is directly under these three bedrooms, right, Madden?"

"Yes," Madden said.

They moved as noiselessly as possible down the great staircase into the vaulted hallway and on into the library.

Kildare crept toward the window, keeping down so that his movements couldn't be seen from outside. Hazard followed him and Madden limped behind. Hazard had just reached the window and was crouched there by Kildare, staring out into the black night, when with the abruptness of a dynamite explosion, there was a terrific uproar somewhere in the blackness beyond the trees. Two mastiffs began bellowing and snarling.

Kildare tensed. "What's that? Sounds like a dog fight. No, it can't be. Those two dogs aren't together. They're—"

His words were cut off by another sound, a sound that filled the interior of the great Italian villa. It was a terrific scream from directly above them on the second floor. A scream of mortal terror and then a choked-off word, "Help!"

CHAPTER 14
DEATH STRIKES AGAIN

AT THE first cry for help, Kildare pushed away from the window. Then Hazard was streaking after him as he tore upstairs through the dark hallway.

They left Madden well behind because of his necessarily slow movements. Reaching the top step they pounded toward the two doors leading to the occupied rooms.

All of the time, Kildare was choking, "We should have made a search of Madden's room after we found the window open. Something was planted inside there. I know it."

"Which room?" Hazard yelled.

Kildare was apparently asking the same question mentally. Then, as in answer to his uncertainty, the door of Powell's room burst open. The boy leaped out, followed by Powell, white-faced and shaking.

"Thank heaven you two are all right," Kildare said. "It must have been Justin. I'll never forgive myself for not making that search."

Then he was pounding at Justin's door and trying the knob. "Justin! Justin! What happened?"

No answer came back to them. A mastiff out in the grounds went into another fit of snarling and barking.

"Maybe," Powell suggested with a frantic hope, "Justin fell asleep and had a bad dream."

"No," said Kildare, "with all this pounding and shouting he would have waked up by now. I'm afraid Justin is dead. And I'm afraid I am the cause of it." He turned to Hazard. "Come on, Jerry. Give me a lift with your shoulder and we'll break in this door."

The two turned sidewise, back to back, strained against the door. Then Kildare moved away.

"All right, now. Back and forth and when I count three put all you've got into it."

"Right," said Hazard.

"One, two, three," counted Kildare.

Together they lunged. The door bent inward, but the lock resisted them.

"It's a heavy one," Kildare growled. "Come on again. One, two, three."

Blam!

The door crashed before their savage attack and the two burst in as wood splintered and the lock pulled loose. Kildare reached for a switch on the wall and swung his flashlight beam about. He found the switch as Hazard's eyes focused on the bed, an empty bed.

Then light flooded the room and four figures turned to stare—four figures that were supplemented that moment by Rocky Madden, who came limping into the room.

"Good Lord," breathed Hazard.

"Apparently," Kildare said, "Justin got up a few minutes ago hurriedly. He must have walked to the window."

He pointed to the place where Justin's body was leaning half out of the window which was partly open. Hazard stared in amazement.

"But I can't figure that out. The man was scared of being killed tonight. Why would he take this chance?"

Kildare shrugged, "I don't know."

"Anyway," Hazard went on, "it couldn't have been your fault for not searching Madden's room."

"No," said Kildare. "Of course that won't bring Justin back to life, but it's rather comforting to know that his death wasn't caused by my carelessness."

"Are you sure he's dead?" Powell asked.

Kildare nodded. "Positive."

"I haven't made any examination yet, but I don't think there's any doubt."

"It must have been something very unusual," Madden said,

"Look out—behind you in the bushes," Hazard yelled.

"that would have drawn Justin over to that window. You remember how nervous he was when he turned in a few minutes ago."

Kildare stepped back to the center of the room, turned to Cappy.

"I wonder if Justin saw the same thing you did. He got out of his bed and—" He broke off, walked over to the window. Leaning over the still form of Justin, he directed his flashlight beam toward the ground. He nodded with satisfaction.

"That's the answer. There's a short club down there below the window."

Madden crowded into the window and stared down.

"That's Justin's walking stick," he said. "He cut it from a tree limb. He must have gotten up when he saw something at the window, seized his walking stick, and rushed over."

Kildare drew back inside. "Yes," he said. "And then it got him."

"What?" Powell demanded.

"I don't know. Possibly one of those lizard snakes like Cappy killed in the kitchen. Let's have a look at him and see if we can find anything."

Hazard stepped forward quickly to help. A strange, eerie sensation took hold of him as his hands grasped that dead flesh of the man's shoulder. They dragged Justin's body back and laid it on the floor. Pulling the pajama top down, Kildare made a hasty, but careful inspection.

"That's funny," he said. "I can't find a mark on him anywhere that might have been made by—" He stopped short and stared at the dead man's throat. There was a slight, bluish tinge there.

"Jove," he breathed. "It looks as though Justin wasn't killed by a serpent, after all. The man was choked to death."

HURRIEDLY, HE brought out a small, folding instrument and a box of powder—his fingerprint equipment. For several minutes, he was still and the others in the room made no remarks. They simply stood staring at him, waiting for him to finish the examination of the marks on Justin's throat. At length, he glanced up with a curious, baffled look.

"That's queer," he said, half to himself. "I can't figure it out. Something climbed up here, climbed right up on the side of the wall outside the villa and there doesn't seem to be anything to cling to."

Madden limped to the window and flashed his light down.

"This wall is pretty rough. I think a small animal like a monkey might get up it."

"That's what I was thinking," Kildare said. "That's what these marks on Justin's throat remind me of. They look like the prints of monkey fingers or toes. You see, there aren't any lines in them like there are in human fingerprints."

Madden frowned.

"This thing has got me going," he said. "I'm going to have a look outside. That ground under the window is fairly soft. I think I ought to find some foot prints there."

"You'd better not," Kildare protested. "There seems to be an elimination process going on here. Frankly, I don't care anything about seeing you take part in it."

Rock Madden jerked his head toward the window.

"Come here, Kildare," he said. "See, the kitchen door is right over there on the other end of the house. You can see it from here. I'll go out the kitchen door. You keep watch from up here. You can turn your light on me and I'll be using mine. I'll be back in a couple of minutes and you can keep your eyes on me all the time."

"You're your own boss, Rocky," Kildare said. "You've been in the service a lot longer than I have and you ought to be able to take care of yourself. But if I were giving the orders, I'd say no."

Rocky Madden jerked his head toward thoughtful, Kildare. "I'll make it all right and I'll feel a lot better after I have a look outside. I feel responsible for Justin's death, anyway."

He limped out of the door and Kildare and Hazard took up their station at the window.

"It must have been something that could crawl up the wall," Kildare said. "See, there are no ladder marks in the earth. I dare say, it's the same thing that Cappy saw at the laboratory window." He stopped, his automatic ready. "There comes Rocky Madden now. See him?"

Hazard twisted and turned the beam of his light on the older government man. Madden had come out of the door and was limping along the side of the house toward them.

He carried his service revolver in his right hand along with his cane. The flash light was in the other.

Kildare surveyed the ground below. There were shrubs growing scraggily along the wall of the house; farther off was open ground.

"Watch out for those bushes," Kildare called. "There might be something in them."

Rocky Madden nodded confidently and glanced up.

"I'm watching."

He reached a point directly under the window and bent over, searching the ground. He laid down his cane as he did so.

"I thought so," he called out after a moment. "There's a foot print down here all right. But only one. It looks as though a baby had stepped in the loose earth and—" They heard him catch his breath.

"What's the matter?" Kildare demanded.

"These other prints. They've got me sort of buffaloed. Prints of two hands, right and left. They are about the size of a man's hand, only the fingers are very long and slim. The thing, whatever it is, must walk on all fours."

Hazard shuddered as he pictured the thing in his mind—a thing with baby feet and hands the size of a man's.

"All right," he said. "Come on up again before it's too late."

Madden nodded. "I want to look these over again."

He was doing just that when it happened.

Hazard suddenly stiffened and yelled, "Look out behind you in the bushes."

Kildare saw it at the same time—a slight movement of the bushes that was barely perceptible. For one second a yellow face leered out; then a tiny thing like a twig leaped through the air. KILDARE POINTED his automatic at the face and pulled the trigger twice. The face vanished. A mastiff dog from the other corner of the house barked furiously.

Then suddenly, Madden was fighting furiously. Shadow boxing, the cop on the docks had called it. That was about what it looked like, as though he were trying to fight off a phantom.

He was struggling to knock something from his body and going round and round as he did so.

Turning, he started running as fast as his bad leg would permit for the kitchen door. But he didn't cry out until he reached the porch steps.

Kildare had whirled from the window by then and was dashing into the hall and down the stairs. Hazard stayed in the window, ready to fire at anything if he got the chance. He saw Kildare dash out of the kitchen door as Madden pitched forward with a strangled cry.

Blam! Blam!

Kildare's gun boomed out in the night. The flame sped over Madden's fallen body toward the bottom of the steps where his flashlight beam had turned. Then Kildare clutched the older man and dragged him into the kitchen.

When Hazard, Powell, and Cappy got down there, they found the lights switched on and Kildare bending over Madden's still form, which was stretched out on the floor. He looked up as they entered.

"It's too late," he said, half to himself. "I warned him."

"He's dead?" Hazard asked with quivering voice.

Kildare nodded.

"Yes. And he was one of the best men that ever worked for the government. They don't come any braver. To think that he would have to go this way."

Powell was staring wide-eyed. "What do we do now?" he stammered. "There are only four of us left."

Kildare's lips tightened. "Yes, it looks as though Wu Fang

were narrowing it down to you, Powell. I think you have less to worry about than any of the rest of us. Wu Fang wants you, but he doesn't want you dead."

He turned now and tried the door to make sure it was locked. Then he came back.

"I think I have figured something out," he said. "I believe that baby-faced thing went up to Justin's window by mistake. Justin saw it and grabbed his club, opened the window and was going to beat it to death when it grabbed him. It must be a harmless enough looking creature."

He picked up the revolver that had dropped to the floor when he dragged Madden in and handed it to Cappy.

"Here, son," he said, "you may need this. Don't hesitate to shoot anything you see moving if you're sure that it isn't one of us four."

Jerry Hazard's nerves had just about reached the breaking point.

"You know," he said, "if I had my way, I'd clear out of this place in a hurry. If Wu Fang is after Powell, why not take Powell with us? We could climb into one of the cars and drive out of here in no time."

Kildare shook his head. "We wouldn't have a chance. Listen!"

The whir of a motor sounded from in front of the house. Kildare dashed out to the entrance hall, snapped on the light and flung open the front door.

His flashlight beam spread across the road where they had left the two cars. He reached for his gun and fired several times in quick succession, but he was firing into the vacant darkness, firing at the backs of two cars being driven away. He turned quickly with a groan and slammed the door, then looked at Hazard.

"I think, Jerry," he said, "that answers your question. Apparently, Wu Fang thought of the same thing you did at the same time, so he's eliminating the possibility of our leaving by car."

CHAPTER 15
THE BABY-FACED BEAST

HE STOPPED stock still and stared at Powell for a long moment. Hazard, watching, thought he was staring at the archaeological chemist as though he were the most valuable treasure in the world, a treasure that had been entrusted to him, and that he was determined to keep safe. After a moment he spoke slowly.

"We've all got to stay in one room and last out this night— if we can. I suggest that we go back to the room where you and Cappy were trying to sleep. I say 'trying' because I noticed that neither of you was undressed when you came out."

"There will be no sleep for me tonight," Powell said.

"I don't think there will be any for us, either," Kildare said, "and it's going to be a long time before morning. Let's go up to your room, then. We'll close and lock the door and keep the window locked. There's only four of us left, so we've got to ride this thing through together."

"Personally," Hazard ventured, "I'd be willing to take my

chances on lighting out the front door and running for dear life."

"Not a chance," Kildare said, shaking his head. "Besides, we've got this little matter of Powell's invention. It would be rather dumb, don't you think, to run away and leave that behind? Let's all go up to Powell's room. We'll sit there and be ready to shoot our way out, if necessary. I have a hunch that baby face will be back and I'd like a good look at it."

Up to Powell's room they went, locking the door after them. Kildare made sure that the window was bolted, then turned off the light.

"We might as well be as brazen about this as Wu Fang is," he said, "and let the yellow devil know that we're all here. He knows we're armed and I don't think he'll be so apt to start anything. Might as well take seats and be comfortable. I don't think we'll have to wait long."

He was right; it wasn't very long before he moved restlessly.

"There's one thing I'm worried about," he said. "It's the crack under that door that leads out into the hall. I don't think we would go wrong if I concentrated my flashlight on it."

So saying he walked over to the door, crouched behind it, snapped on his flashlight, and laid it on the floor.

"Good Lord!" Hazard breathed. "There's enough room under that door for a whole army of these little reptiles to enter."

"It's possible," said Kildare through tight lips, "but I'm not particularly afraid of that. Wu Fang wouldn't dare because he wants Powell alive. Turning those things loose in this room would mean that they would get all of us, including Powell. Wu

Fang is a killer, yes, but he always has an objective in mind when he kills. That isn't why I'm looking at this crack. There's a draft of air coming through it. We made a circuit of this house a little while ago; every window and door was closed and locked then. Now something is open. I think—" his voice fell to a mere whisper—"someone has entered the house. At any rate, we've got three guns. They're going to get a fight for their money. Cappy, you sit over there by the light switch, will you?"

"Yes, sir," said Cappy.

"If I call 'Lights,'" Kildare said, "switch them on. I want them off now because it enables us to see better outside. Let's all get comfortable now. We can't do anything but wait."

That dreaded wait was torturing to Hazard's nerves. He tried to relax. Tried to lean back in his chair. The minutes crawled by like unending hours. No one spoke. No sound came except now and then the rustling of the wind through the trees outside the window.

Suddenly he realized that it was deathly still outside. There was no more howling and barking from any of the great dogs. Had they all been killed by Wu Fang? Probably so, he decided.

The night was still early. It would be quite some time even before midnight, and at least eight or nine hours before sunrise. The thought of sitting here and waiting and listening, with nerves ever tightening, was driving him mad. He got up and walked up and down the room.

Kildare whispered to him, "Sit down, Jerry. I want to listen. Thought I heard something. There it is again."

It was a low, dull, booming sound that echoed through the house.

"A door has been opened," Kildare went on, "and it's banging in the wind." After a long pause, he continued, "I think they have closed it now."

"They?" Powell said.

"Yes," Kildare nodded. "Wu Fang and his agents, they are in this house. Listen!"

HAZARD LISTENED until his ears were ringing from the strain. Then he caught that sound, footsteps mounting the stairs.

Pad! Pad! Pad!

He stiffened. "Good Lord! Can't we do something about it?"

"No," Kildare hissed back. "We made most of the moves tonight. It's Wu Fang's turn."

Pad! Pad! Pad! The footsteps seemed to be coming nearer.

"It's at the door now," Kildare breathed.

Hazard felt those icy fingers along his back again. He wanted to leap out of his chair, race to the door, throw it open, and begin fighting with his bare hands. Anything would be better than sitting here and waiting for he didn't know what. His eyes were bulging and strained on that crack lighted by Kildare's electric torch.

The torch was very dim. He heard Kildare breathe, "The battery is about gone."

That was it. The battery was burning out and any time that beast or human who had crept up to the door might be preparing to slip some of those deadly little serpents in the crack.

The footsteps paused. The room was deathly still. It was still outside, too. Nothing but the wind through the trees, tossing the branches into weird, fantastic shapes. Then, with agonizing slowness, the battery of the flashlight gave out completely and the room was plunged into total darkness.

Hazard jumped up and fingered his own flash, but he felt Kildare's hand on his arm.

"Don't move," Kildare breathed. "I don't think anything is

The thing glared in at them.

coming under that door—not unless Wu Fang has gone completely crazy."

But Hazard was sitting bolt upright on the edge of his chair.

"Good Lord," he breathed, "there's a second man out there. Hear him? They've got us cornered right."

His voice choked on the tail end of that last sentence. Kildare didn't answer for a moment, but he kept his hand on Hazard's arm and somehow, that hand reassured him. A moment later, Kildare released his grip.

"No," he replied, "it was the same one. He's going back now."

Silence fell again over the room. Silence except for the sound of receding foot steps in the hall. Hazard could hear them fade softly, slowly, with maddening deliberation as they moved down the great staircase into the hall below.

Powell's voice broke the quiet. "If I thought it would do any good, I'd blow my brains. That would stop all possibility of Wu Fang's learning the secret I discovered tonight."

"Yes," Kildare agreed, "and the secret would be lost completely. Before you do that, Powell, let's wait a little longer."

They waited for several more minutes. And then, from outside the window, they heard a swishing sound, as though someone were breathing heavily just below the window ledge.

Every eye turned and stared—stared through the darkness. The night was light enough so that from the black interior they could see fairly plainly.

Hazard had watched the trees just beyond sway in the wind, but now something else was coming into their range of vision. Something white that fluttered in the breeze, like a handkerchief. An exclamation escaped Kildare.

"It's a flag of truce! I think that's what it's meant for, anyway."

Instantly, Jerry Hazard was on his feet "You mean," he demanded, "that Wu Fang is admitting defeat?"

"Hardly," Kildare said, "but I think he's about to make us a proposition. Watch the flag. It's coming higher. Somebody is climbing up to the window with it. I think—"

He stopped short as a small, round head appeared over the window ledge. The four occupants of that room sat frozen to their chairs as the round head rose higher, revealing a small, skinny neck attached to a small body.

Cappy gasped, "Gee, that's the thing I saw out of the laboratory window. Shall I shoot it?"

"Not when it's got a flag of truce," Kildare said. "Jove, look at the thing."

THERE WAS an expression of horror even on Kildare's face, for there, perched on the sill, was one of the strangest specimens of flesh and blood at which the eyes of mortal man had ever looked. It was small, perhaps the size of a six months old baby. The body was covered with thin fuzz with streaks of hair here and there. The head and face was that of a baby, although it was pinched and wrinkled a little. The eyes weren't innocent like a baby's stare; they were wicked and gleaming. The legs were short and thick, but the arms were what held the rigid attention of the four occupants of that room. They were long, as long as a man's arms, and much more powerful. Yet the hands were man-sized with thin fingers no larger around than a baby's fingers.

The thing glared in at them for a moment.

Then it raised one great arm and tapped on the window pane. At first, the four men were too astonished to move. Even Kildare sat spell bound. The rapping came again. Then Kildare got up and walked toward the window.

"For the love of heaven," Hazard said, "don't go near that thing! That's what killed Justin."

Kildare nodded. "Yes, I know. But I've got my gun, not a club. At the first sign of treachery, I'll blow the beast's brains out."

The thing hopped along the ledge on those short, grotesque legs and continued to tap on the pane. As it tapped, it looked in to see if anyone were paying attention.

Kildare reached the window. Hazard and Cappy leaped up and joined him; their guns held ready; but Kildare brushed them back.

"I think he carries a message," he said, unfastening the window as he spoke.

His guess was correct. The other arm of the beast came up and held out a piece of folded paper, which it poked into the narrow opening. Kildare took it quickly and closed the window again.

There came a crying, mumbling sound from the beast on the ledge as though it were trying to say something. Then, with a movement so swift that they couldn't easily follow it with their eyes, the thing dropped over the ledge and was gone.

Kildare locked the window, turned quickly with the paper in his hand.

"Light, Cappy," he said.

"Gee," Cappy exclaimed, "I forgot."

He ran to the other end of the room and flipped the switch. As the room became flooded with light, Kildare unfolded the paper.

Come at once to the laboratory. There is something inside the sarcophagus that you have not seen. I have a matter which

I wish to lay before you and which I trust will be agreeable to all.

When all three had read the note, Kildare nodded. "You see," he said. "I told you he was about to make us a proposition." He took out his automatic and examined it, made sure that it was fully loaded. "All right, let's go and see what this is all about."

"You mean," shouted Powell, "that you are going to go right down there in the laboratory and—"

Kildare raised his eyebrows. "Why not? We're in a pretty tight spot. We know very well that Wu Fang can kill all four of us if he wishes. That's why he sent a messenger to find out whether we were all in this room or if it was just a trick. You see, he had someone up in the trees watching and he probably suspected that after we turned off the light here, some of us went into another room."

"Does that white flag mean that he guarantees there won't be any trouble?" Hazard asked.

Kildare shook his head. "No. There will probably be little trouble, though, if we do as he wants. Come on."

With that, he unlocked the door and stepped out into the hall. He turned on the switch that flooded the upper and lower halls and walked downstairs, into the library. The others followed. Suddenly, Kildare stopped.

The library was illuminated and he hadn't turned on the switch. There, on one side of the room, the book case was partly open. So Wu Fang had found the door to the secret laboratory!

Kildare hurried toward it. As he did so, the lights went out, leaving only a dull weird glow that oozed out from the laboratory. Kildare stopped stock still.

"Hazard," he said, "your flashlight."

Hazard's fingers were shaking as he plunged his hand into his pocket. But before he could bring out his flash, another voice filled the room. It had a peculiar, Oriental accent.

"If you wish to proceed in safety, you will not light a light."

There was a sudden movement nearby and then another voice on the opposite side of the room said, "You will place your guns and flash lights on the table just outside the laboratory. If you do not do that, you will be killed instantly."

There was a moment of suspense. Hazard was waiting for Kildare to give orders.

CHAPTER 16
MOHRA

WHEN KILDARE spoke his voice was calm—all too calm for Hazard who was keyed up, ready to blast away with his automatic.

"Of course," he said, "we have taken for granted Wu Fang has invited us to this conference assuring us that we will be safe—at least until the conference is over."

There was no reply. Hazard tried to see the invisible challengers; he thought he distinguished one close behind Cappy. The other he couldn't find.

"You will place your flashlights and your guns on the little table outside the laboratory door," the first voice repeated.

THE CASE OF THE SCARLET FEATHER

Then Hazard got a strange, tight feeling at his throat, for he saw they were surrounded by enemies. An Asiatic had risen from behind every piece of furniture in the room. He couldn't see well enough to tell whether or not they held weapons in their hands, but Kildare had divined the truth. There were plenty of them there. And in that case it would be foolhardy to put up a fight.

Kildare stepped toward the open door through which the weird light streamed; his automatic rattled on the table. Then he stepped back to let the others pass. Cappy came next and laid his revolver on the table.

"Go right on in, Cappy," he said. "I'll be right along."

The boy stepped through the secret doorway; Powell followed and then Hazard.

The latter stared about the little laboratory, nerves tense, muscles drawn up ready for instant action. But the room was apparently empty.

"Do you see anything out of order, Powell?" he asked. For an instant the chemist hesitated, then shook his head.

"No. No, everything seems to be just as we left it. That note told us to look in the—"

He stopped short. He was staring straight at the gold casket and the door was moving. Moving ever so slowly. Opening, apparently of its own will. A long, hairy arm extended around the crack and then something small and naked slithered out.

Powell let out a cry of alarm. Cappy gasped. Hazard was too startled to make a sound. For there, suddenly perched on the

159

top of the sarcophagus was the baby-faced beast. And the rosy face, pinched at the bottom, was leering at them.

The lid was opening faster now. A figure was standing inside of it. The figure of a man in gorgeous silk mandarin coat.

Wu Fang, with hands folded in front of him, and a fiendishly kindly smile upon his face, was staring at them with those strange, radiant green eyes of his. The Chinese spoke softly.

"It is a great pleasure, Mr. Powell, to be your guest."

Powell seemed frozen to the spot. Wu Fang raised one arm and pointed ahead, his weird eyes rolling upward as he spoke toward the baby-faced beast.

"Adolph! You will go out into the library and bring back the feather. I believe it has served its purpose by now."

As Wu Fang spoke he pointed his long-nailed index finger toward the door. The ghastly thing that seemed to be half-human, half-monkey, leaped from those short, stocky, baby-like legs. Leaped straight for Hazard!

Hazard tried to move. But his muscles stuck. The little beast was traveling through the air, long arms stretched out to clutch his throat. Hazard managed to duck.

The next second another figure flashed in front of him. It was Cappy. The youngster was fast—but not fast enough. The beast caught Hazard by the throat and pressed.

Wu Fang was barking a command.

"Stop, Adolph. That is wrong. Let go of the man. He is my friend. I do not wish you to attack him. Not yet."

With that the baby-faced beast let go Hazard's throat and leaped away. Hazard gulped and tried to get his breath. He clutched at his throat, rubbed it to stop that horrible choking feeling caused by those brutal slim fingers.

And when he finally stared down, the beast was gone. Almost instantly it entered the room again, holding in its paw a scarlet feather.

Even now Hazard could smell its fragrant odor; it filled the little laboratory quickly.

Wu Fang was speaking again. His long-nailed hands were clasped in front of him once more and there was a look of benign peacefulness on his yellow face.

"I have asked you to come here, Mr. Powell," he said softly, "to show you something. I know that you have been working on an invention—an invention of fragrant death. I have under my control the only supply of the poison base for your gas that there is in the world. It is here."

Wu Fang moved aside. Behind him five casks were piled, one on top of the other.

"Now I not only offer you these casks and their contents," Wu Fang smiled, "but also an interest in my plan for world supremacy. If you will turn over your invention to me we will work together. We shall perhaps allow Mr. Hazard and his newsboy friend to participate. He, with his newspaper connection, could be of great value."

Hazard's nerves were at the snapping point. Wu Fang had said nothing about Kildare. Wasn't he—

Turning, he looked around. Two half naked, brown-skinned men of Wu Fang stood between him and the door. Of Kildare there was no sign.

"What is your answer, Mr. Powell?" Wu Fang asked gently.
Powell's eyes flashed. "Never. Not if you kill me. Not if you tear me apart. I wouldn't—"

Hazard didn't wait to hear more. He suddenly realized the horrible truth, realized what Wu Fang had meant by saying that the feather had served its purpose.

Ducking low, he started for the outer door. The two half naked men stepped in front of him. He tried to slam past, but he would be blocked even if he succeeded in doing that, for the door to the library was tightly shut.

Behind him all was noise and confusion. While he struggled with the dark-skinned natives, something leaped on his back. Something that weighed fifteen pounds or more. And something fragrant brushed the under side of his nostrils.

Black specks danced before his eyes and then, everything faded and total darkness closed in. He clutched one last recollection before consciousness left him. They were words that came crashing into his dulling senses. Words that were uttered in an angry, screaming voice. It was the first time he had ever heard Wu Fang scream with rage.

AND HAZARD thought of those words instantly upon regaining consciousness.

It was pitch dark about him. It was hard work to even lift himself on his hands; he crawled along the floor, feeling his way. Then he touched something in the darkness. It was a small arm. The arm moved and he heard a low moan.

"Cappy!"

The word left his lips in a hissed whisper. The arm moved again.

"G-Gee!" Cappy gasped. "Gee! Who are you?" There was a weak fear in the voice.

Hazard reassured him quickly.

"It's me, Jerry. You all right? What happened?"

"I—I don't know," said the boy. "Smelled something sweet like flowers and that's all—"

"The feather," Hazard choked. "Thought he killed us. Wait. I'm going to look for Kildare. Are we still in the—"

Hazard glanced up at a lighter blotch in the wall; it was a high, square window.

"Yes," he said, "we're right here in the laboratory."

The boy was moving now, rolling over on his stomach and crawling weakly beside him. They crossed the room to the secret door that led into the library. It was open. Through it they crawled, feeling, feeling. Then his hand touched something.

"Kildare!" he called.

The man on the floor of the library moved. He was breathing hard as though he were having a struggle coming out of an anesthetic.

"Kildare!" Hazard repeated.

The breathing grew weaker and then stronger. Then Kildare's voice answered.

"You, Hazard?"

"Yes." Hazard told him swiftly what had happened. "And the last thing I remember before passing out," he finished, "was Wu Fang telling Powell he would learn the secret anyway. He'd take him and his whole laboratory equipment to his torture chamber in Chinatown."

Kildare forced himself to a sitting position. "Jove," he gasped. "How long have we been lying here?"

"It's still dark," Hazard said.

"There may be time yet," Kildare decided. "We're going to Chinatown."

But they didn't reach Chinatown as fast as they would have liked. It was necessary first to get back enough strength to half walk, half crawl to the nearest house, where they borrowed a car which brought them to Dover in time for the midnight train.

Then a taxi through the Holland Tunnel, across Canal Street, past the Tombs and into the heart of Chinatown.

"How," asked Hazard, "do you expect to find Wu Fang in this tangle of tenements, narrow streets and filth?"

Kildare smiled weakly. The effect of that fragrant feather had only partly worn off.

"I rather anticipated something like this and prepared for it. I have made a friend—an influential and honest Chinaman named Chang Fi. He controls the real estate transactions in Chinatown."

He stopped the taxi at the head of a dark alley, paid the driver. "He lives here," he said as he motioned them out. "I think we'll find him home. Let's go."

The alley seemed clean and free from smells, but it was dark. Pitch dark except for what scant light was shed from a street lamp halfway down the block. Something scurried away at their advance. Kildare strode on.

The alley narrowed to door width at the back. And there was a door back there. Kildare knocked softly on it. From inside came muffled scuffling of feet and then the door opened as far as a chain lock would permit. A dim light streamed out and a fat yellow face peered at them.

"Chang Fi," Kildare said. "I want to know something."

"One minute, please," said the Chinaman. The door closed for an instant and then opened again. "You come in?"

The three filed into a room, gorgeously decorated with thick Chinese rugs, carved vases and massive furniture. Kildare was talking fast.

"Remember what I told you about Wu Fang? That he'd be hunting a place to use as a torture chamber with plenty of underground passages leading to it?"

Chang Fi nodded. "I think he get it. Not sure. You go to address I give you. I send boy to show you right passages. Maybe Chang Fi wrong. You see."

He wrote down the address and handed it to Kildare; then he clapped his hands twice and a Chinese servant appeared. Chang Fi spoke to him rapidly. The servant nodded.

"He know what you want," Chang Fi said. "He only been over a little while—" he grinned mysteriously. "He not speak English yet. He show you."

Kildare nodded and smiled.

"Thanks, Chang Fi. This is going to be a great help. You may be sure we appreciate it."

They entered the alley again and the Chinese servant walked ahead, moving like a shadow.

As they passed the point where the alley widened, Hazard, who drew up the rear, jumped. A hand had passed out from the shadow and touched his arm!

"Please do not go away—yet," a soft voice said.

He recognized it instantly.

"Mohra," he breathed. "Mohra!"

"Shhh," the girl whispered. "Do not let them hear you. Perhaps Mr. Kildare would not want me to talk to you. I know he does not trust me. But you can trust me, Mr. Hazard. You must—"

The dark, exotic beauty drew him deeper into the shadow so that he and she would not be seen if one of the party turned. He felt her warm body touch his for a moment and smelled the faint, alluring odor of the strange perfume that she always used.

"Mohra," Hazard gasped, "I've got you at last. I've wanted to—I've—" he fumbled for words like a school boy—"I want to take you away from Wu Fang. Tonight. Let's go together. Then when I get you safely away from whatever power he has over you I'll go on with Kildare and—"

"No, no," Mohra breathed. "You must not. That is what I wanted to tell you. You and Mr. Kildare. You may think of me what you wish. I have stopped you to say that you must not go to Wu Fang's torture chamber because I—"

She broke off again.

Hazard's whole body was quivering strangely. He couldn't explain it. Didn't care for the answer. All he knew was that he wanted to stay here with Mohra more than anything else in the world.

"You mean," he demanded, "that you're warning me against Wu Fang because you—"

"That," the girl breathed, "does not matter now. I am interested in your safety. I—I—you must not go. That is all. Wu Fang will kill you. He—"

"You'll go away with me tonight, then?"

"No, no," Mohra was sobbing now. "I cannot but you must—"

CHAPTER 17
KEYS TO HELL

JERRY HAZARD suddenly clutched the girl by the shoulder. "Mohra, you've got to tell me some things. I've got to know."

He felt the girl stiffen. "I have warned you. You've got to let me go now. Believe me, you must not interfere with Wu Fang tonight. He is in a violent temper. Promise me that you will go away."

"Not unless you tell me what I want to know," Hazard hissed back.

The girl was trying to push him back, struggling very gently. Suddenly, she seemed to get strength from some higher power and Hazard found himself hurled across the alley. He didn't lose his balance, but he stumbled against the wall. At that moment, Kildare's voice echoed down the passage. "Where's Hazard?"

But Hazard couldn't think of anything else at the moment except Mohra. He caught himself and rushed back to the place where she had been standing, but the dark, shadowy corner was empty. Mohra was gone.

"Hazard, are you all right?" he asked. "Where are you?"

Hazard tried to answer, but his answering words came in a mere husky whisper. He was standing there dumbly, looking at the place where the girl had been. Where he had been a moment ago, holding her close to him.

His reverie was broken by the sound of running feet. Kildare and Cappy were coming back. Kildare stopped and stared at him.

"Lord, man," he demanded, "what's come over you?"

"I—I was just talking to Mohra," Hazard choked. "She's gone."

"Mohra?" breathed Kildare. "Here? What did she say?"

"She said that Wu Fang is violently angry, that we must not go near him or he will kill us."

Kildare snorted. "H'm, that's nothing new. He tried to kill us back there in the Italian villa. What's got him so stirred up?"

"I don't know," Hazard answered. "I tried to find out more but she pushed me away with the strength of half a dozen men and when I regained my balance she was gone."

Kildare stopped stock still for a moment, then jerked his head toward the street

"Forget it; let's go. It's probably some trick of Wu Fang's to keep us away."

Hazard shook his head stubbornly. "I'm sure it wasn't. Mohra did this of her own free will. She was very sincere. You should have seen her."

"I'm glad I didn't," said Kildare. "One of us has got to keep his head. Come on."

He took Hazard by the arm and half led him out of the alley. The Chinese boy was waiting at the street end; without a word, he turned and led them down the narrow sidewalk.

They passed the street lamp, turned to the left at the next corner, walked up a block, and then to the right. Far ahead another street lamp glowed with a dim, dirty light as though it would die at any moment through sheer fatigue.

About a third of the way down the block, the Chinese boy stopped before a building that showed no signs of being occupied. The little shop in the front was vacant; some of the windows above it were broken. There was an eerie feeling of loneliness about the place.

One side of it fronted on an alley which was closed off from the street by a concrete wall about four feet high.

Staring over the wall they saw a little garden. This was not an alley, but more of a court, laid out before a two-story, drab building at the back.

The Chinese servant boy pointed into the garden, nodded significantly, then turned abruptly and moved silently back down the street. Looking closer at the wall, Hazard now saw a door in its center.

"I think," Kildare said, "he means that door is the beginning of the passage to Wu Fang's torture chamber. Let's try."

A GATE in the wall creaked on rusty hinges like a spirit

moaning in the black night, as Kildare threw it open. The three of them passed through.

"Gee," Cappy said, "this would be a dandy place to waylay a guy."

"Yes," Kildare nodded. "It looks very appropriate for Wu Fang's business."

He moved slowly. They reached the house without mishap. The entrance seemed to be a basement one because it opened two steps below the ground. There were no windows on the first floor.

Kildare pushed on the door, which was of heavy oak.

"Locked," he whispered. "There's a keyhole here. I wonder if I have a key that will fit it."

He took out a ring of keys, muffled their jangling sound, and tried several of them.

"No," he said at last, "that's a tricky lock. Well, there's two things we can do. We can either try to break down the door and bring half of Chinatown on our necks or we can wait here until somebody comes. I have a hunch someone will be along soon."

"Good Lord!" breathed Hazard. "We've got to work faster than that, haven't we? Wu Fang has Powell. He's torturing him right now, trying to get the secret out of him."

"I know," Kildare nodded, "but Powell is a pretty stout fellow. I don't think he will tell very easily and we've made good time getting here so far. If we break down the door, we'll be cornered sure as fate. Remember, we're not armed and we haven't got time to assemble an arsenal. We've got to trust to luck for weapons and we've got to surprise Wu Fang. Let's wait at least a few minutes, anyway."

He slipped back into the shrubbery and Cappy and Hazard followed. Suddenly he whispered, "I just found something to use for a club." He passed a heavy round piece of wood to Hazard. "Feel of it," he said. "That ought to do the trick. It's about the size of a baseball bat. I found it here driven into the ground to hold up some shrubs."

They waited several minutes crouched in the dark. Nothing moved about them. Hazard began to get nervous again. He stared up at the broken window panes on the second floor. It seemed to him that he could see figures moving about inside those windows. He clutched Kildare's arm and pointed.

"Look up there. Isn't that a yellow face looking down at us?"

"Where?" Cappy asked.

"Which one?" Kildare whispered. "That window with the two broken panes?"

"Yes. I'm sure there's somebody looking out at us. It's moving. See it?"

"It doesn't look like a face to me," Cappy said.

"No," Kildare said quickly. "It isn't a face. You're letting your nerves get the best of you, Hazard. That's a piece of rag. Get hold of yourself, man."

The next moment Cappy jumped.

"Look! Out over the wall. Somebody is looking at us!"

All eyes turned toward the wall that shielded the garden from the street.

Kildare gasped, "Lord, it does look like the top of a head,

only it's too wide." Suddenly he chuckled. "Confound it, you've got me going, too. That head has four legs. It's a cat. Let's calm down now, all of us, or we'll be half crazy before we get into Wu Fang's torture chamber."

They crouched there in silence. The cat rose up on the wall, stretched itself, and walked to the gate where it jumped down with dignity to the sidewalk and disappeared.

Minutes passed. Then they heard a faint shuffling of feet.

"Here comes somebody now," Kildare said. "Keep down low."

A figure appeared on the sidewalk beyond the wall—the head and shoulders of a slim Chinese boy. He was mincing along through the night. The figure stopped outside the gate, gave a furtive glance up and down the street and then turned quickly into the court. The gate creaked as it swung open. Then the figure was tripping down the sidewalk between flowers and shrubs, heading straight for that door beside which the three men crouched.

Hazard felt Kildare tense, ready to spring at the moment the door would open. But the boyish figure stopped before it reached the door. Words came—words in clear English.

"You are fools, all of you."

IT WAS not the voice of a Chinese boy. It was the voice of a woman—Mohra. "You would not listen to my warning," she went on.

Kildare leaped out and grabbed the girl's arm. "We'll get into this thing now. You fooled Hazard, but you won't fool me."

Something boiled inside Hazard's blood; he clutched Kildare's shoulders and jerked him back.

"Wait, Kildare," he snapped. "You might at least give her a chance to say what she has come to say."

In the darkness, the face of Mohra looked even more beautiful than ever to Hazard.

"Thank you, Mr. Hazard," she smiled. "You are very brave to stand up for me against this blundering fool of a police officer. I have come to help you. But perhaps he does not need help."

"I'm sorry," Kildare growled. "What was it you were going to say, Mohra?"

The girl hesitated. "I don't know whether I ought to give you any assistance or not. You have no faith in me. But I have come to help Mr. Hazard—and you, because you are his friends. I believe you are a man of your word, Mr. Kildare."

"If I give my word," Kildare said, "you may depend on it that I will keep it."

"That is good," said the girl. "Then you must promise me this. It seems that I can not turn you away from this dangerous mission. If Wu Fang gets you tonight he will surely kill you. He is in a bad temper. If I help you, you must promise not to try to detain me. I must be back in less than ten minutes, so I will have no time to argue matters. Do you promise it?"

Kildare nodded. "Yes. I promise it."

"Very well," said Mohra. "Here are two things. Here is a key." She placed that in Kildare's hand. "It is the key to that door," she added, pointing to the one that they had found locked.

"And here," she said, handing a small, white slip of paper to Hazard, "is a parchment. The words are written in code. I do not know what they are myself. Only Wu Fang and a few others

Wu Fang suddenly stopped moving the litter, whirled on Kildare.

in the world know. You must keep it in your inside coat pocket. If you feel it is necessary, present it to Wu Fang with great dignity. But be careful. It is very valuable."

The girl got up from her crouched position in the shrubbery.

174

the **SCARLET FEATHER**

"Mohra," Hazard breathed, "we can never be grateful enough to you for this. I am sure Mr. Kildare has an entirely different opinion of you now."

Mohra didn't answer. She ran quickly toward the gate, passed through it, and vanished beyond the wall.

"You see," Hazard said earnestly, turning to Kildare, "it's just as I told you."

Kildare nodded. "Apparently, it is. That is, if this isn't another one of Wu Fang's traps."

Hazard stared at him in amazement.

"Another one of Wu Fang's traps?" he demanded. "Surely you don't mean that Mohra is helping spring a trap for Wu Fang."

Kildare smiled as he moved toward the door with the key in his hand.

"No," he said, "to be honest with you, I don't, Hazard. I think the girl is sincere. But I do like to kid you about it."

The key made a clicking sound in the lock. Then the door opened. Kildare peered in, jerked his head to Cappy and Hazard.

"Come on. It leads into a passage just as I thought."

They filed in and Kildare closed the door behind them. It was as black as pitch in there. They had to feel their way. No matter how hard they tried to walk silently, their footsteps made weird sounds.

They had gone perhaps ten feet when Kildare, who was still in the lead, said, "Look out! There's steps here."

Cappy was right behind him and Hazard brought up the rear. Down the steps they went. Long steps they were—steps which were made of wood and which creaked as they descended. Kildare was counting them under his breath.

"Sixteen, seventeen, eighteen, nineteen, twenty, twenty-one. We certainly are underground now," he breathed.

Hazard was moving in a sort of mechanical way, his mind

still on Mohra. He was wondering about that strange parchment in his inside coat pocket. What made it so valuable? What was the secret code it was written in? Presently he became aware that the passage through which they traveled smelled musty and damp. It was made of wood planking—old and rotten.

They had been moving along step by step, almost crawling. Suddenly, Hazard bumped into Cappy, who, in turn, had stopped behind Kildare.

"Wait," Kildare hissed. "I thought I saw a light up ahead."

They tensed and listened. Then a sound came to them. It was the first sound they had heard since entering the passage.

Boom!

It was dull and hollow, and yet not loud. It echoed strangely through the rotten wood passage. Hazard's muscles tightened.

"What is it?" he hissed.

"I don't know," Kildare answered, lowering his voice to a barely audible whisper.

CHAPTER 18
THE ORDER OF THE
GOLDEN DRAGON

"GEE," CAPPY hissed, "it sounded to me like a big door closing."

"That's what I thought, but I wasn't sure," Kildare said. "Anyway, we've got to find out."

And now, for the first time, the realization that they were unarmed struck Hazard. Nothing to fight with but that club

Kildare carried and their brains and bare fists. That wouldn't be much against Wu Fang in his torture chamber.

They went on about fifteen or twenty feet before Kildare stopped again.

"That's funny," he said. "The passage widens out here. I think we're in a room."

"I can't feel any sides to it," Hazard agreed as he felt vainly about him. His hands merely groped in space. A horrible feeling of loneliness came over him, a feeling of being suddenly miles away from any reasonable, civilized human beings. He found the tunnel wall again, followed it as it turned out into the room. About five feet to the left, he came to a corner at right angles. He could hear the others treading softly on the board floor.

"Find anything yet?" he whispered.

"Nothing but the wall," Cappy answered. "I'm following it around the other side."

"Sssh," said Kildare. "Don't make any more noise than you have to."

Hazard had turned at the corner and was now moving along the second wall. He guessed he had gone about fifteen feet when he came to another corner. Perhaps it was twenty feet this time to the next corner. Swiftly, he kept track of the shape and size of the room. He couldn't see a thing.

"Let's strike a light and see where we're going," he whispered.

"No," Kildare refused. "We might be seen."

"I haven't found a door yet," Hazard hissed.

"Neither have I," said Cappy.

Now Hazard came to the next corner—the fourth. This room

was nearly square. It certainly didn't have more than four corners. He groped slowly along the wall that should lead him back to the tunnel. He groped on and on, but there was no passage—only another corner.

A horrible thought gripped him.

"Kildare!" he exclaimed. "We're trapped here. I can't even find the place where we entered. Or else this room has five corners, or maybe six."

"Yes," Kildare answered. "I found that out myself a minute ago."

"But what can we do?" Cappy whispered. "We've got to get out of here and save Mr. Powell."

"We do nothing," Kildare said, "except wait."

As he spoke, he was very close to Hazard. Cappy was on the other side of the room. They heard him start toward them, then all three white men froze. From somewhere came the sound of a great gong, echoing and vibrating against the rotten board walls and ceiling.

Bong!

"Where did that sound come from?" Kildare demanded. "Could you tell?"

"I think," Cappy breathed, "it came from that wall I was walking away from. It sounded like it was right behind me."

As he finished, a sudden cry—a scream of torment and fear—echoed through the chamber. It was a cry from the lips of a man in mortal terror. And then, suddenly, short words that were barely audible.

"No. No. Never."

Kildare leaped forward.

"I got it," he said. "Those sounds come from the side of the room where Cappy said. Wu Fang's torture chamber is beyond this partition."

As he spoke, a light appeared as though through the crack of an opening door. Instantly, he pushed Hazard and Cappy toward the corner.

Yes, a section of the side of the room was opening! Someone was coming in. Three heavy wood planks were opening wider and wider. A weird light streamed into their prison, then a shadow was cast across the floor as a figure stepped in.

The instant that the yellow man got past the edge of the door, there was a swishing sound. Kildare's club came down with a sodden thud on the man's head.

Hazard leaped forward to catch the body as it fell. There was no fight in that yellow man now. All stiffness had gone out of his figure and he was as limp as a bag of meal in Hazard's arms. He lowered him quickly to the floor.

Kildare was already pushing toward the door. Another scream rent the air.

SEVERAL THINGS met Hazard's eyes as he tore into that weirdly lighted chamber. It was heavily draped and an enormous gold dragon's head protruded out almost halfway into the center. The eyes of the dragon were gleaming a hideous red. The jaws were snapping together and opening again.

Hung on an elaborate litter halfway to the ceiling, his bare feet toward the dragon's head, was Powell. He was screaming with pain for from the dragon's nostrils, came spurts of searing flame.

Wu Fang stood beside the litter, his back toward the door. His hands were folded in front of him, his head was lifted and he was jabbering something in Chinese that sounded like a prayer to the dragon monster.

Kildare didn't hesitate. He raced for Wu Fang, club raised. As he came within reach of the yellow devil, he swung with all his might. A thud sounded as the club struck, but the fiendish yellow man seemed to divine his danger just before the moment of its execution, for he ducked to one side and the blow that should have knocked his head from his shoulders merely floored him.

There was an angry cry from the side of the room. Kildare tossed the club to Hazard.

"They will be coming," he yelled. "Beat them back. I've got to get Powell out."

Hazard seized the club in mid-air, he whirled as he saw a dark-skinned man leap at him from behind the tapestries. He swung and missed. He brought the club back again and this time he didn't miss. The murderous head flopped back and the body sagged.

"Look out!"

That was Cappy's voice. Hazard spun around to see another figure leaping at him. This was a yellow man, a yellow Chinese servant. He held in his hand an ugly-looking little beast.

As he lunged, he tossed the ghastly beast before him. Hazard's club was ready. It zipped through the air, caught the beast full in the middle, bashed it against the head of the dragon. The club swung again and this time it connected with the yellow man's skull. He went down in a heap on the floor.

Then Hazard leaped to Kildare's aid. The government man had already cut the ropes that bound Powell to the litter and was hauling the chemist across the floor to the door.

"Keep Powell going," he shouted as he grabbed the club again. "Follow me. We've got to get him out."

A brawny, half-naked, ugly man loomed in the doorway. Kildare leaped at him, but there was no space to swing the club. He used it in a different way, like a doughboy would use the butt of his rifle if his bayonet were gone.

The club leaped out lengthwise and crashed against the man's chin. His head snapped back, but he didn't fall. Again Kildare jabbed that club at him.

Wham!

The native was hurled back into the many-sided room, then the club crashed down on his skull. Kildare let out a yell.

"We're in luck. The secret door to the passage is open again. We must have stepped on a trap door or something that closed it. Quick, Powell! Down that passage. Run for dear life! It leads out into a garden. I'm going back and make sure Wu Fang is finished."

Hazard pushed Powell down the passage and turned for a moment, wondering whether he should stay with Kildare or go with the dazed chemist. Then something slammed behind him and he heard Cappy's voice.

"Gee. It's closed again. Powell's gone and we can't go with him."

Hazard spun around. Cappy was right. The door was closed. Apparently, it had worked both ways. Powell, in going out, had stepped on something that closed it. Now they were blocked off from escape.

He heard shouts from the dragon room and rushed back. A horde of brown and yellow men were pouring into the torture chamber. Kildare was swinging his club with all his might. It cracked on the skull of the first man; he sagged limply. But there were more pouring behind him. Kildare was forced to back up.

Hazard leaped forward and struck out with all the power he could command, knocking one yellow man spinning. Kildare connected with another one. Cappy made a flying tackle at one big hulk. The man went down, struggling to beat off the boy.

Everything was a wild bedlam of fighting and yelling. The three white men were giving a good account of themselves, but it seemed that the horde of Asiatics would never end. They poured into the room in a never-ending stream.

Then things began to look foggy to Hazard. Blows were raining in his face; his head was slamming up against the boards. He was fighting with all his might, but it seemed useless. He was still fighting as his legs sagged under him and he went down. But he didn't go out. The babbling was subsiding a little, but the excitement was still there. He was lying on his face, panting dizzily, almost unconscious. His hands were tied behind his back.

IT SEEMED to him that hours passed. The Orientals were standing about, talking. He had no idea where Kildare and Cappy were. Then he was being lifted and carried. He struggled weakly, although he realized there was no use and he decided to save his strength. At least Wu Fang was dead—

Then he stared as though his eyes were going to pop out of his head. For there before him, Wu Fang stood in his yellow mandarin robe. His eyes were gleaming with a horrible green light and he was smiling like a kindly old doctor. He was looking past Hazard. Raising his head, Hazard saw that Kildare and Cappy were being carried in behind him.

The three were backed against the wall opposite the dragon idol, whose nostrils were still spurting flame, and tied there—tied to iron rings set in the wall.

It was then that Hazard called out, for at the other end of the room Mohra was being led in by two beastly-looking yellow men.

"Mohra," he shouted. "Mohra."

Her great, beautiful eyes turned to him pleadingly, but she shook her head slowly.

Wu Fang chuckled. "Ah," he said. "It is as I thought, my little flower. You have developed a great affection for this Mr. Hazard, have you not?"

Mohra didn't answer; she simply stared back at Wu Fang. But Hazard saw her body quiver under the blue gown that she wore.

"I have warned you before, my little flower," Wu Fang went on in his fiendishly kind tone. "Now you must learn your lesson."

He turned to Hazard, Kildare, and Cappy.

"Perhaps you don't understand," he said. "Mohra has betrayed me tonight. Like all bad children, she must be punished. This dragon"—he pointed to the hideous gold head—"is the idol of our secret order, The Sacred Order of the Golden Dragon. Only those Chinese who have attained the highest accomplishments are permitted to belong to this order. This night I have lost my membership parchment. Life holds nothing for me unless I can get it back. The loss demands that the idol be fed. The ritual is quite simple. First, the flames from the dragon's nostrils sear the flesh in order to make it more palatable and then the entire body is fed into the jaws of the dragon and his teeth grinds it to bits slowly, very slowly. A pleasant thought, is it not? Perhaps you are sorry now that you tried to stand in Wu Fang's way."

His eyes gleamed iridescently as they flashed from one face to another of the three who were tied against the wall. Then be turned to the two men who held Mohra.

"You may bind her on the litter," he said in a voice that was horribly kind.

CHAPTER 19
GOD OF VENGEANCE

HAZARD HEARD Kildare's voice ring out. "You yellow dog, you're going to pay for this. You may have us now but—"

That was all Hazard caught. His ears and eyes were closed to all else save Mohra and the two ugly creatures who were lifting her slim body to the litter hanging before the dragon's head.

Frantically he struggled with the ropes that bound his wrists to the iron ring. But the more he fought the deeper the ropes cut into his flesh.

Mohra was struggling too. She seemed to know that now her time had come. Wu Fang had said as much as that. She would be the first one sacrificed at this ritual.

Wu Fang smiled at Kildare.

"You think you have helped Powell escape," he said. "Do not count on that. Very soon he will be brought back here and then—"

The yellow men had Mohra on the litter and were binding her there. They finished as Wu Fang turned back to face the idol and the girl. He lifted his hands into the air, raised his head and began chanting in Chinese.

Hazard was trying desperately to collect his racing thoughts. But it was a tough job. Nothing made sense. They were all going to burn beneath the fiery nostrils of the gold dragon. Mohra already lay writhing on the litter which, even as he watched, moved slowly toward the flames.

Then he remembered the parchment that Mohra had given him. His mind had been such a jumble of insane thoughts during the last few minutes that even Wu Fang's mention of it didn't bring it back to him.

"Stop!" he yelled. "I have something to sell you, Wu Fang."

Wu Fang whirled quickly, leered at him.

"So you are the lover of Mohra?" he challenged. "You do not

wish me to torture her. Why shouldn't I? You say you have something? Only one thing could have any meaning for me now."

"Yes, yes," Hazard agreed. "Stop that litter from moving. I tell you I have what you want. I know where it is. I'll deal with you for it."

Wu Fang made a gesture and the litter stopped its slow movement toward the dragon's head. The Chinaman turned and approached Hazard, who regarded him defiantly.

"If I can get back that parchment of the Order of the Golden Dragon for you," he demanded, "will you release all of us?"

For a moment Wu Fang's eyes glowed like brilliant green lights. Then he tensed and swayed a little, as though he were dizzy.

"Mr. Hazard," he said. "If you are lying to me, I will torment you with the torture of a thousand devils."

"I'm not lying. I can return your parchment if you will promise not to harm Mohra or Kildare or Cappy or me."

"I will make no promises," Wu Fang said. "None except to spare you alone."

Hazard shook his head. "The deal in that case is off."

Wu Fang leaped at him, his long-nailed fingers extended. He clutched the front of Hazard's coat and threw it open.

His hand was plunging into the inner pocket of Jerry's soiled and wrinkled coat. The next second he drew out the parchment

Hazard's teeth snapped as his head dropped. His teeth sank deep into Wu Fang's wrist and he hung on for dear life—gnawed and chewed as hard as his jaws would press.

Wu Fang jerked away. A little of the yellow man's flesh stayed between Hazard's jaws.

Wu Fang stared at the parchment. A look of peace came over his lean, pinched face and he nodded slowly.

"You scrawny rat," Hazard hurled at him spitting the flesh from his mouth.

Wu Fang's eyes were upon him again, glowing more evil than ever.

"For the bite and the names, Mr. Hazard," he said, "you will die with the rest. But I shall save you till last, so that you may hear the screams of the others and watch the dragon's teeth grind their well roasted bodies to small pieces."

Hazard was choking with horror. His eyes roved half insanely about that torture chamber, and fell on certain parts of the decorations. The ceiling and sides were covered thickly with costly tapestries and embroidered hangings. Flimsy things that would burn easily if they were given half a chance. And a sudden, desperate idea came to him.

BUT AT that very moment, when Hazard was about to put his wild plan into motion, Kildare cut in with a similar proposition.

"Wu Fang, you sneaking, yellow rat," he flung out. "You aren't human. The girl has been useful to you and will be again. If you were half a man you'd turn those flames all the way across the room on us. You'd burn us here where we stand. But you can't do that because that golden dragon's head is a synthetic thing with puny little gas jets coming from the nostrils. A poor contraption for something that you say is holy and sacred."

Kildare's voice raised to a bellowing challenge and filled the interior of the torture chamber.

"Turn those flames on us, Wu Fang, and consume us! You think you are all powerful. But you can't do—"

Wu Fang was now pushing the litter slowly toward the flames until the fire began licking at the bottoms of Mohra's bare feet.

Hazard saw her cringe and twist as much as she could under the tight bindings that held her to the draped litter. She turned her great, lovely, tortured eyes upon him. But there seemed to be more pity for him in their gaze than fear for herself.

The yellow fiend stopped moving the litter suddenly, whirled on Kildare.

"I will give you a taste of the heat that you have asked for! You shall see—"

He clapped his hands twice and instantly the two attendants who had tied Mohra to the litter appeared. Wu Fang spoke to them in his native tongue. They took hold of the litter and swung it back. The next second, long yellow flames shot across the room.

As they did so, they naturally curved upward toward the silk drapes and tapestries that decorated the ceiling of the room. Yards and yards of inflammable material up there. If those flames could only get a start in there, then—

Flame hid the rest of the room from his gaze. He heard Wu Fang chuckling; heard Mohra scream and utter his name. But that was all. Then there was a wild cry. A cry in Chinese. But it came with all the sudden alarm of "Fire!"

Others took up the call. The tongues of flame suddenly vanished and Hazard could see once more what was going on.

Wu Fang was racing back to the end of the room. The ceiling was a mass of flames where the dragon's flaming breath had touched. Wu Fang snatched a heavy drape and ran back. His servants began doing the same thing, tried to beat out the flames overhead.

But it seemed that the more they beat them, the hotter they burned.

Hazard was still fighting at his bindings. They would all be cooked alive in there. Suddenly, a small figure darted past him toward Kildare. It was Cappy, and as he leaped, he tore off the last of the ropes that had bound him to the ring.

"I slipped them off one wrist," he choked. "—got to—have your knife, Mr. Kildare."

"Right hand pants pocket," Kildare panted. "Quick."

Cappy worked like lightning. Smoke filled Hazard's eyes so that it was hard for him to see, but he knew that Kildare was free. Wu Fang whirled just before he gave up fighting the fire, saw Kildare and spun around to the litter. Somehow Mohra had struggled almost free of her bonds. She was writhing out of the last rope when Wu Fang, uttering a terrible oath, caught her and flung her bodily into the flames.

Kildare jumped on the yellow devil. Cappy began slashing at the ropes that bound Hazard, freed him.

Jerry Hazard tore into that mass of fire where Mohra had been thrown. He found her and lifted her up from the floor. Then he whirled and rushed out of the flames.

Hands clutched at him out of the smoke and blackness. Hands that led him out into the outer room. And then they were running along the tunnel to the stairs and up into the fresh air of the walled garden.

HAZARD STARTED running across the garden on wobbly legs. He stumbled and went down.

"You're shaky, Hazard," Kildare said. "Let me carry her."

"No," Hazard said almost savagely, "it may be the last chance I'll have to hold her in my arms."

As he dashed out through the gate that Cappy held open for him and onto the sidewalk he looked down fearfully into that lovely face. He thought Mohra's eyelids flickered, but he wasn't sure.

"Kildare, got to get her to a hospital!"

"Yes," Kildare snapped. "As soon as we can. I hear a fire engine coming now."

"There should be an ambulance along with it," Hazard said.

They reached the corner. Hazard stumbled again and recovered. But he knew he was almost finished. Lowering Mohra to the sidewalk, he bent over her as the first fire engine came tearing down the street followed by an ambulance.

The eyelids moved and opened. Mohra was staring up at him. He thought she smiled.

"Are—are you all right—Mohra?" Hazard pleaded.

"Yes," she said softly, "thanks to you. You saved me again, didn't you? I'll never forget that."

"Mohra, promise me that you'll never—"

The girl raised her right arm, placed her soft hand over his lips.

"You must not say it," she said. "Please. Not now. I—I—"

Her lips trembled and she closed her eyes. Hazard shook her shoulder gently, but she seemed to have lapsed into unconsciousness once more.

"Shock and bruises and some slight burns," the doctor at the hospital said. "Nothing serious. A few days' rest and she'll be herself again."

Jerry left his name and address at the desk with orders to call him if anything special was needed for the girl.

When he reached Kildare's apartment, the federal man was getting breakfast in the kitchenette. It was daylight and the sun was streaming in through the window.

"I heard from Powell a little while ago," Kildare said. "He's in good hands. Federal men have him under their wing."

The three sat down to breakfast. Hazard ate nervously. At length, he got up and went to the phone.

"What's wrong?" Kildare asked.

"I don't know," Hazard said. "I feel jumpy. I wish I'd stayed with Mohra. Maybe they've tried to get me at the telephone number I left—and couldn't."

He called the hospital. An excited voice answered when he told his name.

"We've been trying to get you almost ever since you left, Mr. Hazard. The young woman you brought here is gone."

"Gone?" Hazard repeated.

"Yes. The doctor and the nurse were out of the room for not more than two minutes. She seemed to be asleep and when they returned she was gone and the window was open. We've notified the police."

Hazard groaned and said something, he didn't remember what. Then he hung up the phone like a man in a daze.

"Gone?" demanded Kildare when he told him. Then he shrugged. "After all, you didn't expect much else, did you Jerry?"

"I guess you were right, Kildare," he said and his face was flushed with anger. "I wouldn't trust her again if—"

"On the contrary," Kildare said, "I don't feel that way—now. There are some things that neither you nor I nor Cappy can understand. I think I'd trust her more than ever now."

Hazard squared his shoulders and sat down. He nodded dumbly.

"Yes," he said, "I guess so. If you can feel that way, I can. After—everything."

Kildare changed the subject quickly.

"I wonder," he asked, "if any of you noticed what became of the five casks?"

"I saw them piled under the head of the idol," Cappy said. "But I don't know what became of them."

"I don't either," said Kildare, "but I have a pretty good idea. They were burning very nicely when last I saw them."

"What I want to know," Hazard said, "is what became of Wu Fang?"

"That," said Kildare, "is something that only the gods know until we begin searching the ruins of those tenements." He held his hand out to Hazard. "Let me pour you more coffee, Jerry. You need it."

POPULAR PUBLICATIONS
HERO PULPS

LOOK FOR MORE SOON!

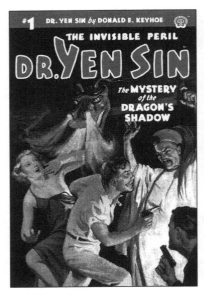